Copyright

1st Edition

Copyright © 2020 Jeanette Coron. All Rights Reserved.

Cover Designer: Jeanette Coron.

ALL RIGHTS RESERVED:

No part of this book may be reproduced or transmitted in any form or by any means, electronic or mechanical, including photocopying, scanning, recording or by any information storage and retrieval system without written permission from the author.

Table of Contents

Copyright

Table of Contents

Introducing the Main Characters

Chapter 1

Chapter 2

Chapter 3

Chapter 4

Chapter 5

Chapter 6

Chapter 7

Introducing the Main Characters

MIKE AND MARY

Mike and Mary are struggling to keep their marriage together as their differences are causing constant conflicts. Mike grew up in the South with his conservative, religious parents, while Mary grew up with a liberal single mother in New York. They both have different expectations of how a relationship should be, based on their upbringing. Mary is romantic, Mike is not. Mary is creative, while Mike is logical and practical. Mary is modern and loves eating out, while Mike is old-fashioned and loves homemade dinners. Mary is organized and hates clutter, while Mike can't seem to ever be able to put laundry in the laundry basket, where it should be. They say opposites attract, but will their differences eventually break them apart? Will they be able to compromise to make their relationship work? Are their differences irreconcilable or can they learn to adapt and save their marriage? Will Mary's constant nagging push Mike away straight into the arms of Carla, his beautiful and curvaceous colleague? Will the trauma they later experience make them or break them? Will they be able to push through the obstacles and difficulties?

LAURA AND JAMES

The Southern belle Laura is married to James a rich successful businessman. Laura and James seem to have the perfect life. They are rich, have a colonial style house with a big backyard pool. They have three beautiful children, Ella Mae, Noah and the older beautiful teenage daughter Allison. Laura is the definition of feminine and is a proper lady who follows etiquette to the fullest.

Using her Southern charm she knows how to get a man and keep a man. She knows that if she feeds her man properly, takes care of the household and herself, then he would never cheat on her. Or would he? Laura knows how to keep a man happy, but is it enough to keep her rich husband from cheating? Is Laura's husband James spoiling her with expensive vacations, spa resort weekends and gifts to distract her from what's really going on? Are their rich, perfect family lives, as perfect as it seems?

JENNIFER AND ANDREW

Jennifer is the introverted, organized, book loving homebody, who is living with her best friend Andrew, whom she doesn't know is in love with her. Andrew is afraid that if she finds out that he is in love with her, it would change everything between them. Jennifer grew up in a strict Jewish household and living with someone who is anything more than just a friend, would be unacceptable. There's nothing Andrew wants more than to be more than just friends with Jennifer, but will revealing his true feelings for her destroy everything? Will Jennifer return his love? Would Andrew be willing to convert to her religion? Would her strict Jewish parents ever accept her marrying a non-Jewish man?

Chapter 1

Men Are from Mars and Women Are from Venus

Mary was on the bed sleeping and she was also dreaming. In the dream she was watching a movie on a cinema screen. In the movie she could see how the screen zoomed in closer and closer to the planet Mars. On the planet there were only men and no women. The men were wearing cave men clothes as if it was an episode of the Flintstones. Everything was a mess and clutter was everywhere. Clothes and trash were lying around in piles and the men were fighting and blowing things up. The screen zoomed towards a man who walked to a fridge and opened it up. The man tore up a milk box, and drank straight from it and spilled the milk everywhere. He then put the empty milk box back into the fridge, instead of the trashcan. He looked around at the dirty unorganized fridge, which contained empty milk boxes, and lots of beer bottles. He then smiled with satisfaction. Then the screen showed something that looked like a bedroom. Mary looked around and was disgusted by the scenery. There was an unmade bed, socks and clothes everywhere, wrinkled shirts and unfolded clothes. "What kind of place is that? I need to get out of here; I can't stand watching this anymore." Mary thought to herself. As soon as she had the thought, it was as if the screen obeyed and started zooming out further and further away from the planet Mars. "Thank God. What a mess and what a place!" She thought to herself as the screen now zoomed in closer and closer to another planet. From a distance it was difficult to see what kind of planet it was. As the screen zoomed in closer to this other planet, she could see it resembled the planet called Venus, it was a planet where there were only women. Then as a scene coming straight out of a Venus shaving commercial, she could see tanned women wearing large white hats, white bathing suits and black sunglasses as they were lying on their white sunbeds. Some of the women were shaving their perfectly tanned hairless legs, while other women were fanning the heat away with their hand held folding fans. The screen then showed a woman who was in the kitchen, opening up the oven and inhaling the delicious smell of a perfect apple pie. The woman took out the pie, put it on the kitchen counter and then admired her perfect edible work of art. She opened up the fridge to find some whipped cream for the pie. The woman looked around at the perfectly organized fridge. Everything was organized after colour and food category. She had heard some rumours about a planet where there existed creatures who put empty milk boxes in the fridge, instead of in the trash where it should be. She had also heard that they put clothes on the floor instead of the laundry box. What a horrible place that must be, the woman thought to herself. The woman then shook off the thoughts about such a horrible place and sprayed some whipped cream on top of the perfect pie. The cinema screen then showed a bedroom with a perfectly made bed and a closet with perfectly folded and ironed clothes, organized after colour. As Mary was dreaming, she was smiling in her sleep as she was admiring this beautiful place where everything was perfectly organized. Her sweet dream and sleep was abruptly interrupted by a male voice.

Waking Up to Reality

Mary felt a strong hand shaking her to get her to wake up. "Mary, you need to wake up. We're going to that place today, it's already 10.30." It was her husband Mike who woke her up. The way Mike had said "that place" told her that he was dreading to go there. She wasn't exactly excited about going to "that place" either. Mary woke up from her beautiful dream to reality. "Already?" Mary replied. "I thought I had set the alarm to wake me up earlier." She yawned as she stretched and put her feet down on the floor. Her long, brown hair was a mess and make-up was still on her face from yesterday, as she had been too tired to remove it the day before. She wrapped her white satin robe around her and put her feet into the pink soft slippers that were right in front of her feet. As she was about to get up to go to the bathroom, she saw all of the clothes that Mike had forgot to put in the laundry basket. "Mike, how many times have I told you to just put your dirty clothes in the laundry basket. It's not like it's rocket science. You just pick up the clothes, open up the laundry basket and drop it in there. If you can drop it on the floor, then you can manage to drop it in the laundry basket," Mary said while looking at Mike who was buttoning his dark blue cotton shirt. "You know what Mary, I'm so tired of your constant nagging, talking to me as if I'm a child and as if you're my mother. I'm a grown man; I should be able to get some kind of respect around here," Mike said clearly angered by her comment. "Respect?" she said also becoming more agitated, as if the word respect had triggered up memories of all of the reasons he shouldn't get just that. Here they started the arguments again. Arguing about something small and then turning it into a big argument about things that had happened years ago. "Respect you say? What about all of the broken promises you've made? You promised me a vacation to France. That was years ago and we still haven't been there. My friends and their husbands have already done so many of the things you've promised me for years. Why is it so difficult for you? And what about our anniversary which you forgot last week? Does that deserve respect?" Mary crossed her arms looking at Mike. "Oh now you want to bring up what happened in the past? You can barely remember where you put your car keys every morning, but you can remember mistakes I made years ago? I'm so tired of being compared to your friends' husbands, how they do this and they do that and how I don't. And I said I was sorry about forgetting our anniversary." Mary didn't look as if she was convinced as she replied. "What about those messages you've been sending to that woman? Does that deserve respect?" Suddenly Mike was silent. He then rubbed his neck and answered with a confused look. "What messages do you mean? Have you been going through my phone again?" he said. "If you want respect Mike, maybe you should try to earn it, instead of making excuses for your behaviour," Mary said and walked out of the bedroom and went to the bathroom to get ready for the day.

On the Road to Counselling

Mike and Mary were sitting in the car on the way to the marriage counsellor they had found. Well it wasn't exactly "they" who had found the marriage counsellor. It was Mary who had done the work of finding this guy who was supposed to save their marriage. In this relationship of two, it seemed as if she was the only one genuinely interested in fixing things. Mike had said that they could fix things on their own, without involving strangers into their life. Well, if he was right, why could they barely talk to each other without arguing? They were both in their own thoughts and they were silent for most of the forty minute drive, until Mike was starting to slow down. He wasn't sure whether he had been driving the right route. He drove slow to see if he could see the address that was on the building. They had GPS in the car, but Mike always insisted on finding addresses without it. This was one of the many things he did which annoyed Mary. How he could never just use the GPS or ask someone for help to give directions. Why did he always have to be so stubborn? "You know you can just turn on the GPS system right? Our appointment is starting in five minutes and we're going to be late," she said as she was looking at her watch and was starting to get impatient. "I will find it without the GPS," Mike said cold. "Well, we would have been there by now if we'd used the GPS," Mary said annoyed. They eventually found the right address and parked in the small parking lot that was there. As they got out of the car they could see another couple also getting out of a car, on the other side of the parking lot. First the man got out of the car and went to the other side and opened up the door for the woman. Then they embraced each other as if they were a newlywed couple who couldn't take their eyes off each other. "Why don't you ever do that?" Mary said to Mike. "Do what?" Mike said being careless, as he knew she would start with the nagging and complaining about what other men did for their women that he didn't do for her. "Open my car door," she said annoyed by his carelessness. "You're a grown woman. You're fully able to open your own car door," Mike said as he locked the car door and started walking towards the marriage counsellor's building. They both rushed into the marriage counsellor's office as they were late. "Sorry we're late," Mary said as she quickly took off her coat and hung it on the coat hanger. "This guy here didn't want to use the GPS, so we could arrive on time." "Well I got us here without it. Didn't I? We're just five minutes late," Mike said as he shook the marriage counsellor's hand and introduced himself. "Hi I'm Mike." When Mary had hung her coat she also went up to the counsellor and introduced herself. "Hi I'm Mary." They both sat down in the couch and were sitting with a slight space between them, as if their body language were saying, "I don't want you near me." Mike was wearing his usual attire of a cotton shirt and jeans, while Mary was wearing her black skirt, black high heels and a white blouse. She could remember it as if it was yesterday, how in love they had been in the beginning and how young and naïve they both had been. Back then they knew nothing about love or relationships, but how they'd learned since then.

How Mary Met Mike

Mary started telling the story about how they had met. She told the story about how she was on her way to her first prom to meet with her then boyfriend John. John wasn't able to come to her house to pick her up, but had told her that she could meet him there at the prom. As she was searching for him through the crowd, she bumped into Mike barely noticing him, just saying a polite "Sorry" as she kept on walking around to find John. What she didn't know was that as she had bumped into Mike, she had dropped her purse. Mike found her purse and tried to get her attention as she was walking towards her date, which she now had finally spotted on the other side of the room. As she was walking closer towards John, she almost thought she saw him kissing her then best friend Ariana, but her best friend would never do anything like that to betray her. How young and naïve she had been, because as Mary was walking closer she could see that they were clearly being closer than they should have. Not only were they close, they were also kissing. Mary felt her heart breaking there and then as the two people who had meant everything to her up until this point were clearly betraying her. Not only behind her back, but also in front of everybody else that was attending the prom. Most people in school knew that Mary and John had been dating for a while and that Ariana was her best friend, and now they were there betraying her with everyone watching. As Mary was walking faster and faster towards them and was about to break them up and speak her mind about what she had just seen, a hand grabbed her from the back and stopped her. "Hi, I'm Mike. You dropped your purse when you bumped into me. I tried to tell you, but you walked away so fast." As mascara tears were slowly coming down Mary's cheek, she tried to keep her composure while she replied, "Thank you." For a few seconds, as she was looking into Mike's eyes, she almost forgot that she had just experienced the greatest betrayal of her life. She quickly remembered again, grabbed her purse and was about to walk towards John and Ariana. Once again a hand held her back. It was Mike again. As if he already had figured out what was happening, he told her "Don't do it, he's not worth it. You deserve better than that. He won't change. If he's done it once he can do it again. Why not find somebody who respects you too much to do that?" As tears were running down her cheeks, she tried to speak without crying, but weren't able to. Mike just hugged her and held her tight. What she didn't know was that Mike had a crush on her and finally had the chance to hug the woman he was in love with. He hugged her and didn't let go until she had calmed down. What they didn't know was that as they were hugging each other John had spotted them both, not knowing that Mary had already seen him kissing her best friend. John pushed Mike away from Mary and said, "What are you doing with my girl?" Mike looked at Mary and pointed his fingers at her and said to John, "Maybe you should ask your girl why she's crying? She saw you kissing Ariana, and see how you've made her feel. You don't deserve her, she's a good girl. She deserves better than that." A few tears were running down Mary's cheeks as she was telling the story of what had happened years ago. The whole experience had been heart breaking for her, but something good had come from it; her relationship with Mike. That night they had walked out of that place together holding hands. Mike had comforted her and protected her in the most heart-breaking moment of her life, and that meant a lot to her. That night she didn't know what to make of them holding hands, all she knew was that she didn't want to let go of his hand. "He didn't let go of my hand until he had walked me safely home to my front door. He hugged me, and then I went inside," she said to the counsellor who was sitting in front of them. How much things had changed from those innocent teenage years, to now sitting here talking to a stranger about their problems hoping he could fix it. Mike had been reluctant at first, and as a man he thought he could fix things himself. As a woman she thought talking it out would help. They had been married for 5 years now, but she was just beginning to learn how different they were, and how different men were from women. Mary continued telling the story. "That night after the prom he had been so attentive, respectful and protective over me, I had no doubt that he would be a good boyfriend and even a good husband in the future, but I just hadn't been ready. I had just experienced heartbreak and ended a relationship and I just wasn't emotionally ready for a new relationship. We talked and kept in touch over the phone for a while, but eventually the communication between us just faded." Mary kept telling the story about how fast forward ten years later, destiny happened. Mary had been at a restaurant with her girlfriends eating a nice meal when she had to go to the ladies room. As she was about to walk, she bumped into someone. "Oh, I'm so sorry," she said. She looked up and looked into the eyes of a man that seemed familiar, but she wasn't quite sure if it was who she thought it was. "Mike, is that you?" she said. With a surprised but happy look they both recognized each other. They hugged and from that moment they were almost inseparable. That night they had walked around the city together talking about everything that had happened since they had seen each other as teenagers. He had told her how he had met a woman and been in a relationship with her for many years and how it didn't work, and she explained that she recently had ended her relationship with a man she had met many years ago. They both had experienced heartbreak and both had their own good and bad experiences with love. It could be so difficult to open up your heart again after a break-up, but it had been so easy with Mike. She felt like she could trust him with everything. He made her feel safe. "That was back then, but now things are different," Mary said to the marriage counsellor. Everything had been good until she had found that message on his phone. She could remember that day clearly, how Mike had left his phone on the living room table and gone to the bathroom. Mary was sitting on the couch in front of the table when Mike had received a message on the phone. She had an internal conversation with herself wondering whether she should check the phone or not. She had been in relationships before where she had been betrayed and her trust issues got the best of her and she checked the message. By the time Mike had come back to the living room the look on her face had changed. "What happened to you?" Mike said, clearly noticing the change in her mood. "Nothing," she said cold, not looking at him. She got up from the couch and quickly said to him, "I'm tired, I'm going to bed." Mike was used to her mood swings by now. There was always something he did wrong, he felt like he was never good enough for her. She always talked about her best friend Laura and her husband James, how he always bought her flowers, how he took her to those expensive resort vacations, that he himself could not afford to spoil her with. Of course he wanted to, but he just wasn't there financially, he was not a millionaire like James. Not being able to provide her with the things he knew she desired made him feel less of a man and insecure, it didn't help that she made more money than him either. He also felt like she didn't appreciate him, and all of the things he did do right. He showed up to work day after day, paid the bills and was doing the best he could do. He knew about men who didn't care about their women at all; at least he was trying. There had been this new woman at his job who seemed to notice everything he was doing right. She laughed at all his jokes and made him feel good enough and appreciated, why couldn't Mary do that? That woman, his colleague Carla had asked for his number so he could help her if something needed to be fixed or repaired, as he was hired to fix computer errors. It had started with that, but lately she had sent more text messages, always caring about how he was doing. He couldn't remember the last time Mary had asked him how he was doing. Instead she was always nagging about everything he did wrong and he was starting to get tired of it. He remembered how lovely and pleasant Mary had been in the beginning, never complaining about anything. Now it seemed like nothing he did was good enough for her. "It would be nice to be appreciated once in a while, but all I'm hearing day in and day out is what I do wrong, and what I don't do right," Mike said to the counsellor. "I used to think that I could trust him, but I don't trust him anymore, not after I saw those messages from that woman," Mary said. Mike sat for a few seconds in his own thoughts, going through in his mind, every message that she might have seen. Could it be this message or the other one? He didn't know, because she didn't want to say. "You keep talking about this woman and these messages, but you don't want to tell me which woman and which message you've read. What were you doing in my phone and checking my messages anyway?" Mike said. After the marriage counselling that day, they both felt like they had done nothing but remind each other about everything that was wrong about their marriage. It was difficult to see how they could turn things around and make their marriage good and healthy again.

Lunch with the Girls

Mary needed to get out of the house and get a break from all of the things that was going on between her and Mike. That's why she had made lunch plans with her friends. The girls had gathered at their favourite lunch spot as they often did. Sheila was late as usual and the girls were waiting for her. Being unsurprised, the punctual Jennifer shook her head and said, "Nothing unusual about her being late." Jennifer couldn't understand how it could be so difficult to arrive on time. Jennifer was Jewish and she had long brown beautiful hair and a flawless body. She was working at a successful business, while dealing with pressure from her family. She had always prioritised work before love and didn't have any children. Her parents thought she should focus on finding a husband, get married and give them grandchildren. Jennifer had met Mary in college and had introduced Mary to her close friend Sarah. Sarah was the successful African American friend who had built up a million dollar cosmetic business and always had free cosmetic to give away. She was married to Eric with whom she had two children Jeremy and Chloe. Her husband Eric also had his own successful business and they had the kind of life that many only could dream of. Her close friend Trina was also at the table which Mary now had also known many years through her friendship with Sarah. Trina was an African American, and a tom-boy who was the opposite of Mary's best friend, the Southern belle Laura. Trina could care less about figure shaping underwear, high heels and wearing make-up. She was a single mother working on raising her teenage son and working on achieving her dream of opening up her own restaurant. She currently worked at a restaurant as a chef. The Southern belle Laura had been Mary's best friend since college. She had long blonde hair and a charming smile that could win the hearts of anyone. Laura had moved from Tennessee to New York to study at the same college as Mary, and as different as they were they still managed to become friends.

Using her Southern charm Laura had managed to get herself a rich husband at a young age, getting pregnant shortly after the wedding. She was now a housewife, working fulltime with raising the three children Ella Mae, Noah and her beautiful teenage daughter Allison. Her rich husband James spoiled her with expensive gifts, flowers and vacations. She was obsessed with etiquette and often commented on the other girl's lack of it, and still no one has ever seen her outside of the house without make-up. When she first moved to New York from Tennessee, Laura's mother had worried about her being in New York alone. She had then asked Barbara whom she knew from the South, to watch over her, and make sure she was doing okay in the big city. Through Laura Mary met Barbara. Barbara was the oldest lady in the group with a lot of wit and wisdom. She was never afraid to speak her mind and often did so without thinking before she spoke, which gave the girls a lot of laughs. She was three times divorced with grown children and was currently single, which she enjoyed through going out with her much younger friend Sheila. She met Sheila through her job as a saleswoman and introduced her to the group. Sheila was the youngest in the group. She was the young, blonde, single, party girl who worked as a sales woman. She was known for being chronically late and often clashed with Jennifer who was the opposite of her in every way. As the girls were waiting for Sheila to arrive they started chatting. Laura the Southern Belle of the group was wearing a pink dress, high heels and had perfectly manicured nails. She was staring at Trina which was biting her nails, something she often did when she was nervous. Laura couldn't help but to stare at Trina's nails, and couldn't help but to say something. "You know what Trina? I know this lady which can give you an amazing manicure. I can call her right now if you want." Trina looked at Laura with a confused look. "A manicure, what do I need that for?" As the tom boy she was, she couldn't understand what manicures were practical for.

She had tried it a few times and could barely keep the nail polish on for a few hours before she damaged the manicure through doing some work using her hands. Manicures and working as a chef chopping vegetables weren't exactly a good match. "Well maybe if I had a rich husband who did all the work and paid all the bills, I could sit around and look beautiful with manicured hands too, but I don't have that luxury. I have to work for a living, to keep a roof over my head," Trina said to Laura. Laura pretended to be shocked at the bluntness and rudeness of Trina, but she had gotten used to it by now. "Maybe if you took better care of yourself you could have had a rich husband too, but when you refuse to listen to sound wisdom, then I guess you get what you deserve," Laura replied. Eventually Sheila arrived rushing in to the restaurant saying "Sorry I'm late guys. I want to come up with a really good excuse for being late, but I don't have any." She sat down and put her purse and jacket on the table. Not exactly a master in etiquette she broke all of the etiquette rules of Laura, who knew that a proper lady doesn't do that. She found it difficult to keep her mouth shut, as she wanted the best for the girl and to teach the girls to be proper ladies like she was. Mary, knowing Laura too well gave Sheila a warning. "Hey Sheila, you better find another place to put your purse and jacket before the etiquette expert comes for you," Mary said while pointing her fingers at Laura. "What me?" Laura said pretending to be surprised by the comment. After the girls had ordered their lunch and drinks, Mary was ready to share what had been happening with her and Mike the last few weeks. "So... me and Mike are trying marriage counselling," Mary said. The girls seemed surprised. They knew that Mike and Mary had struggles in their marriage, but not that it had come to this. "I found a message on his phone from a woman at his job," Mary said to the girls. "What kind of message?" Sarah said. Sarah had been texting on the phone until this point, but now she turned her attention to the conversation as she had experienced something similar in her own marriage a few years ago. Laura the "marriage expert" in the group tried to figure out what Mary had or hadn't done, for this to happen. "This never happen if you follow the proper rules and etiquettes," Laura said to Mary, thinking about her long marriage. Laura had known how to keep her husband happy all these years and had never experienced him being unhappy in their relationship. "This is what I've been trying to tell you all these years Mary," Laura said. "I tried to warn you, if you're too ambitious, make more money than him and let him see you without make up in the morning, this is what happens." "Wait a minute here. You mean you've never let your husband see you without make-up?" Trina said to Laura. "No never, not even when I was getting surgery. I put on my best clothes and make-up and never let him see me with that hideous blue surgery cap. He wasn't allowed to see me before my hair and make-up was properly done after the surgery," Laura replied. "I don't know what kind of education you get where you're from, but that's crazy," Trina said as she shook her head. Mary continued to talk about what had happened. "Well I think he's cheating, but I'm not sure," Mary said as she looked at the girls. Barbara came up with this bright idea. "Well what if we stalk him to see what he's really doing. I have a new car; he won't know it's us."

Mary Stalking Mike

Mary got up early the next morning and got out before Mike was going to work. "I'm going out for a walk," she said to him as she was walking out the door. She walked a few blocks away where the girls had parked the car. She looked around to see if anybody saw her getting into the car and quickly got in. Barbara was in the driver's seat, while all of the other girls were sitting in the back. Mary sat down in the front next to Barbara. All of the girls were wearing dark glasses and head scarves as a cover. "This is so 'not' unusual or suspicious at all," Mary said sarcastically. "Whose idea was this disguise anyway?" It was Mrs. Southern Belle over there," Trina said pointing her fingers at Laura. "Well at least y'all look like proper ladies now," Laura said with her Southern accent. "Here's one for you too Mary," Laura said and handed Mary a scarf and a pair of sunglasses. "I can't believe you guys talked me into doing this." Mary was surprised at herself, for doing what she was about to do. But she had experienced cheating before and wanted to know the truth, before she gave anymore of herself to this man she had spent so many years with. "Well what are you going to do if it turns out he is actually cheating on you. Will you stay with him or will you leave him?" Trina said. A bit caught off guard by the question, Mary didn't know what to answer, as it hadn't really dawned upon her until now that maybe she would see something she didn't want to see. She could feel her stomach turning, but she couldn't stop now. She had to find out. "Well as the woman here with the most relationship experience, I have a few advices for you," Barbara said. "You want her to get relationship advices from you? You've been divorced three times," Laura said horrified. "Exactly!" Barbara said. "I should know more than anyone here; what to do and what not to do. I've learned a lot from all of my marriages and divorces," Barbara said and then took a pause as if she was about to reveal something she wasn't really ready to share. "Girls, I have something to tell you. I know you see me as the fun party girl of the group, and the one here who enjoys single life the most of us, but I have to be honest with you. I hate it," Barbara said with a sad look on her face. The girls were shocked at what Barbara had just revealed. She was the one in the group who seemed to have the most fun and enjoy life the most. They often jokingly called her Mrs. Robinson as she was the oldest lady in the group, and her long blonde hair and curvaceous figure, tight dresses and high heels often caught the attention of younger men, which often gave the girls something to make fun of. Barbara wrapped her white fur scarf around her neck and continued: "It gets lonely, you know, and I'm not good by myself. I was always looking for something better in my relationships, someone better, but let me tell you, the grass isn't always greener at the other side. And suddenly you end up in your 50's single and dating one idiot after another, and then you realize that there is no perfect guy out there," Barbara said with a sad look on her face. "Sometimes you have to take what God gives you, even if it is a guy with flaws and all." Barbara sighed as she took a sip of her coffee. "Or a guy who leaves empty milk boxes in the fridge and leaves dirty socks everywhere except for in the laundry box where it should be," Laura said and shook her head. "What? James does that too?" Mary said slightly shocked. "He doesn't look like the kind of guy who does that, he seems so polished and organized." "Well guess who irons his clothes and keeps him organized?" Laura said. "Me of course. He's a man too Mary, they all do it. It's in their genes. It's the man-gene," Laura said as she sighed. "Men, can't live with them, can't live without them," Sarah said after she had been quiet for most of the conversation. "Why are you so quiet today Sarah?" Trina asked. Sarah took a deep breath before she explained, "This whole thing just reminds me about something me and my husband Eric went through a few years ago. It was difficult, but we got through it, for the children's sake. I couldn't stand him for a long time after he had cheated on me with that woman. I didn't want him to be close to me. I didn't want him to touch me, as I knew where his hands had been. I pretended to love him in front of the children for a long time, just for the children's sake. I thought I'd never get over it, but eventually I just did. It took a long time though. It isn't easy, getting over such a betrayal, but eventually I learned to love him again." Suddenly they saw Mike's car driving out from the driveway. Barbara drove after him and followed him down the road. He took a turn and was driving towards Queens; something which Mary thought seemed unusual. "This is not where he usually drives to work. He doesn't work in Queens, he works in Brooklyn," Mary said a bit confused. When Mike came to a neighbourhood with lots of brick houses next to each other, he started slowing down. Not long after that, he stopped close to one of the houses and parked there. As Mike parked the car a woman came out of the house, locked the door and started walking towards his car. Mary had never seen that woman before; all she knew was that she looked beautiful. She had long silky black hair, was wearing a white tight blouse, black pencil skirt and black high heels. As the woman was walking closer to Mike's car Mary could see her face more clearly, she could see the red lipstick she was wearing and how she was smiling at Mike as she entered the car. After that they drove off. All of the girls were in a state of shock, so much so that they almost forgot to follow them. "Well drive after him Barbara!" Trina said. "I'm starting to get nervous about this," Barbara said. "I did this with my first husband, and it didn't go very well," she said nervously. "What happened?" Mary wanted to know. But before Barbara could answer Mike stopped the car at a gas station and walked out of the car. The girls froze and was sure that he had seen them in his rear view mirror and was about to come to their car. Luckily for them he instead went to the back of his car. He opened the trunk and took out what looked like a gift and brought it to the front and gave it to the woman sitting next to him. Then

Mike went into the gas station alone, while the woman was waiting in the car. Shortly after that he came out with flowers in his hand and opened the passenger door and gave it to the woman. He got back into the car and started driving. Mary was shocked. "He bought her flowers?" she said. "This is the guy who can't even remember our anniversary or remember to buy me a gift on my birthday. But he can do that for a stranger, for another woman?" She shook her head. There was no way to misinterpret what she had just seen right? There could be no other explanation other than that he was cheating on her? Eventually Mike arrived at his job and he and the woman went inside the building where Mike worked. "So what do we do now?" Mary asked. "Sit here for 8 hours until he's done working?" "Of course not!" Barbara said. "Now we install a tracking device on his car." The girls looked at each other and said, "You're not serious are you?" "Of course I am," Barbara answered and got out of the car. She went to the back of the car, opened the trunk and started sorting through all of the things she had there. "Oh, here it is," she said happy to have found what she had been looking for. "I'm just going to put this thing on his car. I'll be right back," Barbara said and then walked small, but quick steps in her high heels and tight pink dress towards Mike's car. She then put something under his car. After that she went back into her own car and started driving away from the parking lot. "What was that? What did you do to his car?" Mary asked. "I just put a tracking device on his car which alerts me on my phone when he's driving and also shows me where he's driving. In case he wants to go somewhere else but home after work today."

Waiting for the Alert

The girls had driven home to Barbara's house, and were sitting there drinking sweet tea which she had served. Barbara's phone was in the middle of the table and the girls were waiting for it to beep any minute now, as Mike was about to finish work. The phone gave an alert sound which made Mary spill some of her tea on her shirt. "I have to change my shirt," she said. "No there's no time for that, we have to go now," Barbara said as she pulled Mary's arm, and they all went out to the car. They were all sitting in the car driving as they were looking at Barbara's phone which showed the route Mike was driving. "He's driving towards Queens again," Mary said looking at the map on Barbara's phone. The girls drove after Mike and parked behind him. He had once again parked his car outside the woman's house. The woman went out of the car alone and went inside of her house. Mike was still in the car. "Hmm... seems like he was just dropping her off at her house and nothing more," Laura said. "But why is he waiting in the car, why isn't he driving?" Mary responded. Suddenly she saw the same woman come out of the house again. "Look guys, she's coming out of the house and she's walking towards Mike's car." The woman walked towards Mike's car, but didn't enter. Instead Mike came out of the car and they started walking down the street together, to a small restaurant on the other side of the street. Then they went inside. When the girls were sure Mike couldn't see them, they went down the street to a bench on the other side of the restaurant and sat down there. Barbara was carrying a case, which she now put on her lap and opened it up. "What in the world is that Barbara?" Laura said. "Just a few tools I've saved from some of my previous marriages," Barbara answered. "Now let the pro do her work," she said looking down at the briefcase which contained binoculars. She took them out of the briefcase and put them in front of her eyes, and steered the binoculars in the direction of the restaurant were Mike and the woman were sitting. "Oh my!" Barbara shouted. "What happened? What are they doing?!" the girls said. "I zoomed in on some dog on the other street. It was a scary looking dog. Sorry," Barbara said. The girls sighed out of relief. Barbara finally steered the binoculars in the right direction and saw Mike and the woman. "Oh," Barbara said. "What's happening?" Mary said wanting to know what he was doing. "They are just talking," Barbara said almost as if she was disappointed and had expected to see something else. "Let me see," Mary said and took the binoculars from Barbara and into her own hands. She saw them both in the binoculars. Mary studied the interaction between Mike and the woman and watched their facial expressions as they were talking. Mike seemed so happy as he was smiling and laughing. Mary wondered what the woman was saying to him, to make him seem so happy. She couldn't remember the last time she had seen him like that. The whole situation made her feel sick, and she just wanted to go home. "I've seen enough," Mary said as she was putting down the binoculars. She started walking towards the car and the girls quickly hurried after her. "Why are you walking away?" Barbara said. "Don't you want to see if they do something more?" "No." Mary said and went into the car and closed the door. The car ride back to Mary's house was a quiet ride. The girls wanted to cheer her up, but didn't know quite what to say. The message alert sound on Mary's phone broke the silence. "Mike sent me a message. Saying he will be home late today."

Moment of Truth

Mary was waiting in the living room and was sitting in front of the television, with a large ice cream box on her lap. She was eating straight out of the box. She was switching through the television channels. She landed on an episode of "Cheaters" as a victim of cheating was given the evidence of their partner's cheating. The victim and the camera crew were sitting in the car getting ready to confront the cheater and the partner in crime. They stormed out of the car to where the cheaters were standing and confronted them. The host pointed the microphone to the cheaters and explained how they had been following them around and knew that they had been cheating and asked questions about their relationship. Not long after there were fighting and shouting. Mary turned off the television. This wasn't how she wanted her story to end; she wanted a fairy-tale, not being in her own version of a cheaters episode. Not long after that Mike entered the house. He took off his coat and shoes in the hallway and came into the living room and sat down next to her. "Hi," he said as he attempted to give her a hug. "Please don't," she said as she pushed him away. She could smell the perfume of that other woman. "What have I done now? And don't say 'nothing', as you usually do. I can't read your mind you know. We can't fix things if you don't talk to me," Mike said. "It's nothing," Mary said and looked at him with an angry face. "Well you say you want to fix things, but how can we fix things like this?" Mike walked out of the living room and went upstairs to the bedroom. Mary turned on the television again and landed on a sermon with a preacher. Once again thoughts about ending her relationship with Mike were sneaking into her head. She didn't know how much more she could take of this emotional rollercoaster. As thoughts of frustration were growing inside Mary's head, the preacher on the television said a few words of wisdom. "The grass isn't greener on the other side; you have to mow that grass too."

Fighting Again

Mike had gone to his job early and Mary had a day off. Mary wanted to be productive, but could only think about how Mike was with that woman at work all day long. Thoughts were running through her head, would Mike take that woman home today too? Would he take her out to restaurants or even worse? Her heart was beating faster with every thought. She had to find out who this woman was. She went to her computer and googled the woman's name. She had seen her name on Mike's phone. She wrote the name "Carla Ortiz" in the search bar. Lots of different women came up. It seemed like there were many women out there with the name "Carla Ortiz". Mary felt sick just thinking about the other woman. She scrolled through all of the profiles until she finally found her. There she was. That husband stealer. Mary clicked on Carla's profile and scrolled through her page trying to find out information about her. She looked through her photo's seeing if she could find a photo of Carla and Mike together. If she was to confront Mike about this, she needed something, some kind of proof. Suddenly the door opened and Mike entered. "I'm home early," he said. "I went to work earlier so I could come home to watch the game." He went to the kitchen and found a bag of snacks and brought it to the living room. Mike sat down in the couch, not noticing Mary frantically trying to turn of the computer which had frozen, with photos of that woman all over the screen. Had it been a laptop, she could have just closed it and brought it with her upstairs or somewhere to fix it, but this was a stationary computer with a big screen in the middle of the living room. Mary tried her best to sit tall, as to cover the computer screen. Mike was noticing that she was acting weird. "What are you doing over there?" he said. "Nothing," Mary said obviously unconvincingly so as he started walking towards her. "What is this?" he asked. "Why are there photos of my colleague Carla all over your computer screen?" He crossed his arms and was impatiently waiting for an explanation from Mary. "I know about you and that woman," she said. "I know about your dates, your car rides, the messages and the flowers." Mary was getting more and more emotional and agitated as she remembered all of the things she had seen. "I know everything!" she said barely being able to control her emotions and as tears were coming down her cheeks. "Everything?" Mike said, slightly raising the tone of his voice. "What dates, what flowers and what messages are you talking about?" he said as if he knew nothing about what she was talking about. Mary was getting more agitated as he pretended like nothing had happened. "Don't lie to me and pretend like you've done nothing. I've been there too many times before Mike, and I'm not doing it again." "What do you mean Mary? I have been nothing but faithful too you all these years. I am not your ex. Do not compare me with the guys you've been with in the past, because I'm not them," Mike said. "Well if so, what were you doing with that woman at her house in Queens and at the restaurant close to her house?" Mary answered. "First of all, I don't know how you know all of this. Second of all I was helping out a colleague. She's new at the job; she doesn't have a car and asked if I was driving past her neighbourhood on the way to work, as it took her a long time to get to work without a car. I told her I could pick her up, even though it wasn't on my driving route to work. I was just being kind, helping out a friend. Had it been my male colleague, you wouldn't have said anything," Mike said getting angrier. "So do you buy gifts and flowers to your male colleagues also?" Mary said in a sarcastic tone. Mike didn't say anything. He just walked out the door and slammed it. He then went into his car. Mary could hear him open and slam the car door. Not long after that he came back inside with a gift box and flower in his hand. "You mean this gift and these flowers which I bought to you?" Mary was confused and didn't know what to say. "I asked Carla if she could help me with finding a nice gift to you.

She said I should buy you these flowers and this gift." Mike handed Mary the gift and flowers and then went upstairs to the bedroom and closed the door. Now Mary felt bad. She had let her trust issues, suspicion and jealousy get the best of her. She opened the gift which was a necklace with her name inscribed on it, and felt even worse. Mike hadn't been cheating, he had been telling the truth. She felt foolish for going so overboard with the stalking and so wrongly misunderstanding the whole situation. She went up to Mike slowly walking into the bedroom, feeling guilty and ashamed. "So... I saw the gift. The necklace... It was beautiful," she said as she sat down on the bed beside Mike. He was resting his head with his arms behind his neck, staring up at the wall, with an angry face. She turned to the side staring at Mike trying to get him to look at her. He didn't look at her. "Did you see the inscribed name on the necklace?" he said with an angry tone, still not looking at her. "Yes," Mary said. "Was it her name or your name on that necklace?" Mike said cold. "It was mine," Mary answered. "We can't continue like this Mary. Your trust issues are wearing me out. You're checking my phone, my messages and even going to the extent of stalking me around. I can't live like this," Mike said and eventually got out of the room as he said, "I'm sleeping in another room tonight." Mike went down to the living room to sleep on the couch. As he wasn't able to sleep he turned on the television which turned on to the sermon channel which Mary had been watching the day before. The preacher quoted a Bible scripture. "Because if a man has even just lusted at a woman, he has committed adultery with that woman." Mike looked up towards the computer screen which still was frozen with images of Carla. He looked at them for a few seconds until he went to the computer and unplugged it and went to the couch, trying to get some sleep.

Mike Visits His Friend

Mike and his best friend Thomas were sitting in Thomas's basement, or the "man cave" as his friend Thomas liked to call it. They were drinking beer and watching sports on television. They were both shaking their heads as they were talking about women and took a sip of their beer. Mike started explaining what had happened the day before and how Mary seemed to have stalked him and his colleague around town. "Women do many strange things, but what were you really doing with that woman? Are you sure there's nothing going on between you?" Thomas said. "Maybe it was wrong of me to go to her house and go out to eat with her, but it was so refreshing to have a woman make me feel that I'm good enough. Carla, she's always laughing at my jokes as if I'm the funniest guy in the room. If I fix or do the simplest things, she compliments me and makes me feel like I've done something great. I can't remember the last time Mary made me feel that way. It's always nagging, nagging and more nagging. 'You don't do this or you don't do that, you don't take me to France on vacation, other husbands do that for their wives.' It's like I can't do anything right when it comes to Mary, and I'm honestly tired of it," Mike said frustrated. They were both shaking their heads and took another sip of their beer. "Women, can't live with them, can't live without them," Thomas said. Thomas could relate to what Mike was going through. "The nagging is the worst. I just can't stand it. I mean I'm a grown man; I can put my clothes where I want to. The house doesn't have to be perfect every second of the day, you have to be allowed to live and breathe in it too. Sometimes I think she wants the house to be like a museum, you can only see, but not touch anything there," Thomas said as he sighed out the frustration which had been building up. "Women can't live with them, can't live without them," Mike repeated as he was drinking his beer. They continued to eat snacks and drink beer, with their feet on the table. The table was filled with empty beer bottles and they had dropped chips on the floor. "You know I'd be in trouble if my wife could see this mess right?" Thomas said. "Definitely," Mike answered. "The good thing though, is that this is my man-cave. I'm the boss here and I make the rules. No women and no nagging are allowed in this place," Thomas said proudly as he carelessly dropped chips on the floor. "I should get myself a man-cave too," Mike said.

Chapter 2

Laura to the Rescue

Laura was vacuuming up the snacks that had fallen on the floor around the living room table, and was picking up the empty beer bottles her husband James and his friends had been drinking while watching sports the night before. Then her phone rang. It was Trina. Trina rarely called Laura for a girl talk, as they were as different as they could be. "Trina?" Laura said. "Hey Laura. Yes it's me. I know I don't usually call you and I usually don't do this, but I need your help," Trina said. "You need my help?" Laura said confused. "What kind of help?" She continued. Trina started explaining how her date Nick had been starting to lose interest in her. They had been dating for months, but the last few weeks he barely cared to text back or asked how she was doing. Now this wasn't the first time this had happened, so Trina was starting to take this personally. What if it was something that she was doing wrong? And would it really be that bad trying to take some of the advice Laura had been giving her. Trying to be a bit more feminine, and trying to follow the proper "ettequette", or what was that word again? "Etiquette, that's how you say it," Laura said. "Laura, I need you to help me be a better woman. I really don't want to lose this guy, I really like him. You can do whatever you want with me, whatever it takes to make me be better. I will do it if you help me," Trina said. Laura could barely hold her excitement; she loved make-overs and had wanted to do a make-over on Trina for a long time. "I thought you'd never ask," Laura said ecstatically.

Laura and Trina were walking in the mall and searching through dresses to find one for Trina. Trina couldn't remember the last time she had been wearing a dress or anything pink, or anything with a heel on it, but it was worth a try. Laura wanted her to wear exactly that; a dress, something pink, and something with a heel on it. The higher the heel the better Laura had said. "The first thing we need to do is to get rid of those pants. It's time to get you into a dress," Laura said as she found different dresses to put on Trina, but she realized that Trina didn't have the flat stomach she herself had, so she quickly went and found some shaping underwear for her to wear. "Here take this," Laura said handing Trina figure shaping underwear. "I can't breathe with this thing on," Trina complained after she had put on the figure shaping underwear. "Stop being such a drama queen. Just suck it up buttercup, like the rest of us do," Laura said. But sucking it up was the last thing Trina did when they went to the waxing place. "Ouch, that hurts." Trina screamed as the waxing lady was removing the hair from her legs. "No man is worth this pain." She complained. After they had gotten Trina's nails done at Laura's manicurist they went back home to Laura's place. Laura got Trina seated in a chair in front of a mirror and started putting make-up on Trina. "I'm starting to look like the black version of Dolly Parton soon if you continue to put on more make up," Trina said looking in the mirror as Laura was happily applying make-up on Trina's face. Laura applied the finishing touches on Trina's hair and make-up and Trina eventually became more pleased as she got used to her new look. "I almost don't recognize myself," Trina said with a face that showed a mix of not being sure whether she liked it, but at the same time being pleased with having a different look. As Trina was admiring her new look, Laura looked at Trina and started to preach about Southern etiquette. "Now a proper lady, never sits with her legs spread. Like I've seen you do on several occasions," Laura said with a face that showed slight disgust with the thought of a woman sitting in such an un-feminine position. "A proper lady always wears lipstick and mascara; she never leaves the house without it. She doesn't raise her voice, she speaks softly and gently. She doesn't show too much ambition, and she never tries to compete with a man. She's selectively helpless and selectively clueless..." Laura said and was then interrupted by Trina. "Selectively helpless and clueless?" Trina asked, questioning if she had asked the right person for help. "I said I would do anything, but I won't do that. That is an insult to my intelligence. Are you saying you want me to pretend to be less smart than I am, to please him?" Trina asked. "Do you want this man or not?" Laura said. "Yes," Trina answered. "Then you must do this. Trust me this works," Laura said. "A man loves to feel like he's the smartest one in the room; he loves to be needed and to fix things. If you do this you will make him feel like a hero. Let me demonstrate with a story." Laura started telling the story of how she had gotten her husband James to marry her. "So I let the car lights stay on the whole night on purpose, knowing that the next day I couldn't start the car. I called James as I already had his phone number, and I asked him if he could help me with my car. Of course he said yes, as men loves to fix things, and of course I was wearing my best outfit when he came over to fix my car. He fixed my car and I thanked him with some sweet tea and delicious baked goods. I had also already prepared dinner and made him my Southern comfort mac-and-cheese special, the recipe my grandmother gave me, the same recipe she used to get my grandpa. As you know a man's heart is through his stomach. He was mine there and then. I never let him know though, that my father taught me how to jump start a car when I was a child. He still doesn't know that," Laura said with a smile. "What, wait a minute. You know how to jump start a car?" Trina said. "Of course I can. A smart lady always knows how to fix things herself if she has to," Laura replied with a confident smile. "Well, enough of the chatting now. Go and show your man what he's missing out on if he leaves you," Laura said and started cleaning up the make-up they'd used.

The Man Cave

Mike had invited his friend Thomas over to help him build a Man-Cave. They were in the basement of the house and were making a lot of noise, when Mary came home from work. Mary came down to the basement holding her hand over her ears as to block out the noise. "What in the world is going on here? What are you doing? What is all this noise?" Mary said irritated. "I'm building a man-cave," Mike said proud crossing his arms as he was looking at his friend who fully supported his decision. "A man-what?" Mary said. "A man-cave," Mike said again as he smiled at his friend who was there to support him in building his cave and also supporting him in standing up to his wife, whom he knew would oppose his plans and ideas. Mike explained, "A man-cave, is a place where men can get a break from the nagging of the women in their lives. A place where men can just be men. A place where a man can feel like he's the boss and make his own rules," Mike said. Thomas showed his support to Mike's plans. "It's a place where women aren't allowed, so maybe you should go upstairs and bake some cookies or something. Tell her Mike," Thomas said seeing the offended look on Mary's face. Thomas already knew that Mary didn't like him and they had stopped trying to be polite to each other. "Yes I'm fixing this place so I can have a place to go to when I need to have some... man-time," Mike said awaiting the predictable irritated reaction of Mary. "What do you need that for?" Mary said irritated. With Mike having his friend supporting him, she knew it was two against one. She knew this was Mike's friend Thomas's fault; he had given Mike this idea. She didn't understand how Thomas's wife was able to put up with him for even a minute. She let out a sigh of frustration and walked back up to the living room and called her friends. She told them about Mike's plans to build a man-cave, she didn't want the basement to become a victim of male destruction. She imagined how Mike would turn the basement into a place of complete clutter, dust and disorganization. She was sure he just wanted a place where he could make a mess, and mess up the perfect order she had in the house. She needed to stop this horrible plan. She first called Laura who told her that "she just needed to let Mike be a man and build a man-cave if he wanted to." That wasn't what Mary wanted to hear, so she called her next friend Sarah who also didn't understand why it was such a big deal. So she called her next friend Trina, the strong independent woman whom she knew would understand her and had her back in this thing. "Girl, you need to stand up for yourself." Trina advised. "You can't just let him boss you around," Trina said gesticulating with her hands as Mary nodded in agreement through the phone. "Yes you're right Trina; I need to stand my ground. I'm going to make myself a "she-shed", a place that's all pink, all organized with no men and no clutter allowed," Mary said pleased as she had come up with a game plan.

Mary had found another room in the house to turn into a "she-shed" as she called it. She had found a box of pink paint and was in the process of painting the room. Mike was on his way to the kitchen, when he suddenly saw that Mary was painting the room pink. He stopped abruptly. "What in the world are you doing with this room?" he said. "I'm building a she-shed." Mary said proudly as she continued painting. "A she-what?" Mike said. "A she-shed, a place where there's no clutter and no men allowed. A place I can go when I need a break from all of the cluttering of male species," she said. "What is it with you and this need to compete with me all of the time? Can't you just let me have this one thing for myself? You need to stop with this feminism and 'whatever-a-man-can-do-a woman-can-do-too' attitude of yours, because it's not working for you," Mike said not impressed with her she-shed plans. Why couldn't she just be happy with a traditional role as a wife and just let him be the man of the household? He was so tired of this feminism thing. "Why is it a problem that I am independent and able to do things for myself?" Mary said holding a hand on her hip. "Because sometimes you just need to let a man be a man," Mike said and left the room and went to his man-cave in the making. "Why does everybody keep saying that!" Mary said as she continued painting.

Laura Becomes Suspicious

Laura was sitting at home in the living room drinking some sweet tea, when her husband called. When she answered the phone he explained that he would be late from work, again. It had been often these last few months. Before that it was long in between and he was always home in time for family dinner with the children. These days it seemed as if work was more important. She knew that with certain other women who didn't follow the proper rules of how to keep a man happy, that could mean cheating. But she had followed the rules, done all of the things a woman should do to keep her man happy. She always looked her best, never let him see her without make-up or her hair undone. She always kept his stomach happy through making homemade dinners every day and was often baking, filling the house with wonderful aromas. She always kept her house clean, tidy and as beautiful and pleasant as it could be. When he wanted to watch sports with his friends she lovingly served snack and beer and something good to eat. She didn't nag him and she had let him be the man of the household. She kept thinking through all of the things she had done to keep him happy at home, with her. She had agreed to be a stay at home mom and a housewife, taking care of the children and the house. She made sure that she didn't make more money than him, was ambitious or did anything that would intimidate him or make him feel less than a man. She went through a check list in her head, and she had check marked them all. She couldn't think of one thing she hadn't done right, so she shrugged of the thoughts about cheating as nonsense. She grabbed her thousand dollar purse, got into the car and went to the mall to do some shopping. When she arrived at the mall, she went to her favourite store to buy a new dress. She knew exactly what kind of dress her husband liked, and maybe she just needed to give her husband something more exciting to come home to. Laura looked through the beautiful dresses as she bumped into another woman who was also looking for a new dress. "Oh excuse me," Laura said." She looked at the other woman who looked like she came straight out of a movie. She looked flawless in her tight white dress, long blonde hair, and fit body. The expensive jewellery she was wearing made her look like a rich model or movie star. The woman looked at Laura with a blinding white smile. "No problem." The woman turned and walked away towards a man that was waiting for her. The man kissed her and put his arms around her as they walked away together. What the man didn't know, was that his wife Laura had just witnessed him cheating on her with another woman.

Laura sat at home later that night and was in a state of shock, as she had just a few hours earlier witnessed her husband cheating on her with another woman. By the time her husband came home that night Laura was a wreck, she had never thought this would happen to her. She thought her husband would be as faithful to her as her father had been to her mother. She thought her husband would be remorseful and repentant when she confronted him with his sinful behaviour, but she had been mistaken. She had been waiting for him in the living room; her hair and make-up was a mess. Her mascara had been messed up by all of the crying she had done secretly upstairs in the bathroom, as the children had been in their rooms getting ready to sleep. She sat in the living room chair with a drink in her hand. Her husband opened the door and walked in and hung his coat in the hallway unsuspecting of his wife's knowledge and mood. He entered the living room and saw Laura. "What happened to you? What's with you hair and face?" he said surprised. Laura replied as she put down her drink and stood up. "What happened you ask? You and that woman is what happened. I saw you, I saw you both at the mall, kissing. I was there James," Laura said as she was sure he would start to beg and plead and ask for forgiveness, but his tone was different than what she had anticipated. "Laura, you know we've been struggling in our marriage for a while. There's no love or romance between us anymore, it's not what it used to be. This woman makes me feel alive; I feel a kind of love for her that I haven't felt for you in a long time." Laura was shocked; she didn't know what to say. She had to sit down to keep from fainting. All she knew was that she had to get out of the house. She couldn't stand being in the same room as this man that was supposed to be her husband. She wanted to throw the glass she was holding at him, at the floor or the wall or anywhere, just to make a statement. Thinking about her children sleeping peacefully upstairs, she took a deep breath and instead slowly put the glass down at the table beside her. She walked slowly towards James and stood in front of him; she looked at him for a few seconds before she slapped his face. She then took her purse, went out to her car and drove off.

Laura Breaks Her Own Rules

Laura had never thought she would ever be the kind of woman who went to the store without lipstick, mascara or even high heels. But here she was in the store, looking like one of those women, who did just that. She hated herself for failing herself like this; not only herself, but generations of women before her. What would her mother say if she had seen her? She would have been ashamed. "A woman never leaves the house without looking like a proper lady." Her mother had preached over and over again as she grew up. She had never been happier to be in a big city and far away from her mother and the people who knew her parents. Had she been in the South in the small town she was from, the news about her looks would have spread faster than wildfire and eventually reached her mother. Thankfully she was here in a big city where she wouldn't see anyone she knew. It wasn't long after the thought had entered her mind, before she saw a group of women she recognized. It was her friends. It was Trina, Sarah and Jennifer. What were they doing there? They didn't usually shop in this store. She tried to hide between the food shelves, but managed to bump into someone and then bumped into the food shelves making products fall on the floor around her. Not only had the girls now noticed her, but the whole store. The girls came up to her. "Laura is that you? We almost didn't recognize you. You look different today," they said. "By different, you mean ugly right? I'm not wearing any make-up," Laura said as if all of her confidence was in the make-up she usually wore. "You're not wearing make-up?" Trina said. "You the 'never go to the store without make-up' preacher. This is not like you. Are you okay?" Trina asked. "I want to say yes and pretend like everything is perfect, but to be honest, everything is not perfect and everything is not okay," Laura said and took a deep breath before she explained what had happened. "James has another woman. It's been going on for a long time. It's so serious that he's considering a divorce. He's willing to break up our home and family and break our children's hearts, for her. How can he do that?" she said as she started crying while her friends were comforting her.

Carla Invites Mike

Mary was sitting in the living room as Mike was in his man-cave. There had been a lot of tension between them lately and she had barely seen him since he made his man-cave, a place where he had been sleeping often the last few weeks. He had forgotten his phone and left it one the table in front of her. The phone was making a message sound and lit up, and Mary was thinking about letting Mike know that he had gotten a new message. She was about to take the phone and walk down to him when another message, and a message from Carla was showing on the phone screen. She looked at the message. *"Hey Amor. I miss you. I will be waiting for you at the party tonight. I'm looking forward to seeing you handsome. Kisses and hugs, Carla."* Mary felt the anger rising within her. So she had been right all along, there was something going on between them. She walked back and forth trying to figure out what to say, what to do and how to confront Mike. She didn't think for long before she went down to the basement where Mike was and confronted him. "So you're going to the party tonight huh, with Carla? Well I hope you'll both enjoy yourselves together then!" Mary said and threw Mike's phone hard on the table. "Hey careful with my phone and what are you talking about? Are you starting with this Carla thing again? And why are you checking my phone again?" Mike said as he was also getting angrier. "So now you want to pretend like you don't know what I'm talking about?" Mary said and picked up the phone again and read the message out loud. "Hey Amor. I miss you. I will be waiting for you at the party tonight. I'm looking forward to seeing you handsome. Kisses and hugs, Carla." Mike had a look of shock on his face as if he didn't know how to react or what to say. "So now I know there's really something going on between the two of you!" Mary said as she started crying. Mike was clearly uncomfortable and didn't know what to say. "Well...uhm... I don't know what to say Mary. I'm so sorry you had to see that. But I promise, there's nothing going on between us. I don't know why she's sending me these kinds of messages," Mike said. "So now you're going to pretend like nothing has happened between you, even with this message and evidence? You really think I'm that dumb. I've been there and done that before Mike, and I'm not doing it again. I didn't marry you so you could go and be with other women. I'm leaving," Mary said and started walking. "Mary, please don't go," Mike said as she was walking away. Mary went up to their bedroom and started putting clothes and make-up in a small suitcase with Mike following after her trying to talk to her. "Mary, please talk to me. I promise, there's nothing going on." Mary put her hand up towards his face and said, "Don't talk to me." She then took her suitcase, went downstairs and out to the car and slammed it.

Andrew Has Something to Tell Jennifer

Jennifer sat in the living room on her couch, working on her laptop as usual. She was unsuspecting of what was about to happen next. Little did she know about Andrew's plans and what he was about to do. They had been best friends and had shared an apartment for a long time. They had met in college and then out of economical conveniences they chose to move in together. Jennifer's parents were strict Jews and wouldn't have approved of her moving in with a man she wasn't married to. Back then she was young and rebellious and did the opposite. She didn't let her parents know, and she wasn't worried about living together with her best friend Andrew. She knew that there was nothing between them romantically anyway. He was kind and he looked okay, and yes they got along great, but she didn't think of them becoming anything more than friends. She already knew that her parents wouldn't approve of it if she would choose to get into a relationship with him anyway, as he wasn't a Jew as she and her family was. Andrew looked Jewish though, with his dark hair and olive skin, but looking Jewish and being Jewish were two different things. What she loved about him was that just like her, he also was a homebody, an introvert who loved to stay at home and who disliked parties. He was good company on the weekends, when everybody else was out having fun. She didn't have anything against parties, she just enjoyed being at home more than she enjoyed being out. That was more enjoyable to her than going out getting drunk, seeing people fight, and sweaty old guys hanging over her trying to hit on her oozing with the smell of alcohol. Being at home was more her thing; and she had to admit that she was grateful for Andrew being there to keep her company. He came into the living room and brought snacks and sat down beside her. They had already chosen a movie to watch for that weekend. They sat close as they often did; he put his arm around her which he often did, so she didn't think anything about it. What he was about to reveal to her next, she however, did not expect. Andrew was nervous, as he was about to reveal something big. He was afraid of Jennifer's response and of what would happen to their friendship after he had said what he was going to say. He straightened up a bit, adjusted his glasses and looked at Jennifer. "We've been friends for a long time Jennifer, and I appreciate our friendship so much. That's why I'm a bit nervous about what I'm about to say next." Jennifer suddenly became more attentive to what he was saying and looked at him. "I'm afraid that saying this might ruin our friendship, but I can't hide these feelings any longer. I can't imagine living without you Jennifer, you mean so much to me. I love having you as my friend, but the truth is that I want to be more than just friends with you. I have feelings for you; feelings I can't hide any longer. The kind of feelings that makes me imagine you as my wife, spending our lives together and growing old together. I've tried to suppress these feelings, but they keep coming back and keep growing stronger every day. I can't even look at you anymore without thinking about how much I want to be with you." Andrew paused slightly trying to decode Jennifer's facial expression before he continued talking. She was quiet. "Jennifer I love you, and I'm scared to say that. I know that after I've said those words, we can't go back to normal, pretending like I didn't share my feelings for you. That's why I'm hoping you will say that this isn't just something I'm feeling, that this is something you feel too, that the feelings are mutual." He took a deep breath and was waiting anxiously for Jennifer's reaction. She paused as to take in all these things that he had revealed to her. She froze for a bit and didn't know what to say. "Andrew… I… don't know what to say…" she said and became quiet for a while. Her slow response made Andrew nervous. Maybe he had ruined their friendship forever; maybe he had misunderstood what she was feeling for him. How she didn't mind it when he sat close to her, put his arms around her, how they spent almost every weekend together watching movies and not being out with everyone else. How she sometimes looked at him. Maybe he had misinterpreted all of the signs that said that she also had some kind of feelings for him as well? Maybe it had been just wishful thinking? "Andrew…" she said with another slight pause. "I don't know how to say this…" Andrew already knew that this wasn't the response he wanted to hear. "Andrew. You know I love you very much, as a friend. I was just thinking how grateful I am to have you, as my friend, but I don't think we should ruin this. Our friendship is so good, and we're so good together, as friends." The way she was emphasizing the word friends, made him understand that that's all she wanted, to be just friends.

Marriage Counselling for One

Mary was sitting on the couch alone. "I don't know how we got to such a dark place in our relationship," Mary said to the marriage counsellor. She took a slight pause before she continued. "But one thing led to another. He did things to hurt me, and I wanted him to know that I could do things that could hurt him too. I remember standing in front of the mirror looking at myself putting on make-up, and checking out the new beautiful dress I had bought. I put on perfume, my high heels and I took my purse and went to the hallway and put on my coat. 'Where are you going?' he said from the living room. 'I'm going out to eat dinner with Richard,' I replied as I went out of the house and locked the door. I went to the car and drove off before he managed to say anything more. Shortly after that I was getting message after message. 'Where are you going? What do you mean you're going to dinner with Richard?'" Mary shook her head as she realized how damaging that moment had been to their relationship. "I then went to a restaurant with Richard that night. Nothing happened between us. We were just friends and colleagues. I had just done it to make him see that I also had options if I wanted to. I have to admit it; yes I was petty and yes I was wrong in doing it, because it seemed to be the last straw which destroyed our relationship." Tears were coming down Mary's face as she was retelling the story of what had happened. "Eventually the jealousy and the trust issues between us became greater than the love that used to be between us. How can you be with someone you don't trust?" Mary sighed. "So that's why you're here alone today?" The marriage counsellor asked. "Yes," she answered.

Andrew and the Friend Zone

Andrew and his friends Eric and Thomas were sitting at a restaurant. They had found an outdoor table to sit by and were chatting as they were waiting for their food. "So she turned you down, just like that?" Andrew's friend Eric asked. "Man, that's cold-hearted," Thomas said while shaking his head. "I really put it all out there, everything I am feeling for her. Then she said that she wants to be just friends," Andrew said. "Now she has you locked up in that friend zone for real," his friend Eric said. Eric was Sarah's husband and Andrew had met him through Jennifer and Sarah's friendship. "Ah the friend zone, many men have entered it, but not many have been able to escape," Thomas said. "Let's have a moment of silence for all of the guys out there stuck in the friend zone," Eric said and bowed his head while pretending to be sad. "What is the friend zone anyway, and how do I get out of it?" Andrew said frustrated. "I was in the friend zone once," Thomas said. "She said she wanted us to be just friends and that she wasn't ready for a relationship at the time, and a few hours later she was posting love and relationship quotes on her social media. The friend zone is frustrating man, it's like a prison," Thomas said and took a sip of his beer. "What happened? Were you able to get out of it?" Andrew asked, hoping to get some clues. "No, I just stopped having women as friends, and the problem was solved," Thomas answered. While they were talking they saw a young boy and girl walking past the restaurant. The boy was carrying the girl's purse and shopping bags, while the girl was chatting on her phone about how wonderful another guy was. "Now that guy is really stuck in the friend zone. Poor guy," Eric commented. "Well how do I get out of this friend zone thing?" Andrew asked; still hoping to get some answers on how to win Jennifer's love and get her to want to be more than just friends. Eric the self-proclaimed "dating advisor" of the group answered. "If you're stuck in the friend zone it can mean one of two things. Number one: She likes your personality, but she doesn't think you're attractive. Number two: You're making it too easy for her to be able to get you, and you've never given her the chance to miss you or see that you can get other girls if you want to. In other words, do your best to look your best. Don't always be available when she calls you, give her some time to miss you and let her at least think you have a life and other things to do besides sitting around waiting for her. Let her see that you have other options out there," Eric said. "You mean I should date another girl?" Andrew said as if it was the wildest idea he had ever heard. A message on his phone interrupted his thoughts. "It's from Jennifer," he said to his friends as he was about to reply. Eric stopped him and took Andrew's phone from him. "So we've gone through the theory, now it's time to practice what you've learned. You're not going to reply to her for at least two hours," Eric said as he saw the look of shock on Andrew's face. "For two hours? I can't let her wait that long. She was wondering if I could buy some milk on the way home and..." Andrew said as Eric interrupted him. "Do you want this girl or not?" Andrew paused and said, "Yes." "Then you got to follow the rules and do what I've taught you. You got to give her time to miss you," Eric replied. After a few minutes Andrew got impatient, thinking about Jennifer who was waiting for his reply. "Can't I just reply her now?" he said. "No," Eric replied firmly protecting the phone from Andrew who looked ready to try to take it any minute to text Jennifer. "Come on man, give me my phone now," Andrew said. "No," Eric said while scrolling through Andrew's phone. "Don't scroll through my phone, that's private." Andrew protested. "Aww," Eric said as he scrolled through Andrew's photos. He continued looking through Andrew's phone and laughed at some of the photos. "It's not funny. Give me my phone now. I won't text her okay?" Andrew said. "Promise?" Eric said. Andrew couldn't promise that he wouldn't so he didn't answer, but instead quickly grabbed the phone from Eric's grip. He started texting on his phone as the guys were shaking their heads. "He's impossible; he's going to stay in that friend zone for a long time."

Mike Confronts Carla

Mike knocked on Carla's office. "Hey Carla, can I talk to you for a second?" he said. "Yeah sure Mike, what can I do for you?" she said with a smile. "Look Carla, I don't know if you might have been getting mixed signals from me, but you know I'm married right?" Mike touched his neck feeling uncomfortable with the situation. "Yeah, I know Mike," Carla said. "But you don't seem to be too happy in your marriage though. You know I'm here if you need anything," she said looking straight at him. Mike took a deep breath before he replied. "Carla, I don't think it's appropriate that you send me the kind of messages you sent me. My wife saw them and let's just say that she wasn't exactly happy about them. It got me in a lot of trouble," Mike said to Carla who was staring at him. "I didn't mean to get you in trouble Mike. Next time I will be more careful if that's what you want," Carla replied. "Carla, what I mean is that…" Mike's phone rang and interrupted the conversation. "I have to go and take this phone. We will finish this conversation later," Mike said as he was on his way out of the office to take the call. "I'm looking forward to it," Carla said unbothered with a smile.

Chapter 3

Marriage Counselling for One

Mary sat at the couch looking down in the cup of coffee she was holding. "So that's why you're here alone today?" the marriage counsellor said to Mary before taking a sip of his coffee. "Yes, I wasn't ready to tell Mike about what happened in my previous relationships. But I have to be honest; I was very close to being petty and doing the same thing again. But now I know the damage it can do to a relationship, and I don't want to lose Mike. I just can't, I love him too much. He's different. He may not be romantic, he may have a few flaws, but he's different from the other guys I've dated and been in relationships with. He's different in a good way. What can I do to fix our relationship? How can I make him happy again? How can I make him laugh and smile, as I saw him do with that woman?" Mary said desperate for a healthy and positive change in their relationship. The marriage counsellor looked at her. "Let me tell you something which many men won't tell you about themselves. We men love to be needed. When a woman are what you ladies call 'strong and independent', it makes us wonder where do we fit in your lives. We need to be needed; we need to feel like the man in the relationship. We also need to know that we are valuable to you women and know that we are appreciated. Our love is different. We show love by doing small things as fixing things around the house and paying the bills. You want him to show you that he loves you, which he does; he just does it differently. Look Mary, I suggest you start complimenting him on the small things he does. If he fixes something in the house compliment him, and show him that you appreciate it. Try less nagging and try to give him some more space. Try that for a few weeks, then you can come back and tell me how it went." As Mary was driving back home from the counsellors office, she was thinking about all of the wonderful years she and Mike had been together, and tried to figure out when things had started to go wrong. Had she really been nagging too much and was she the one who had been pushing him away and into the arms of Carla? Could she really fix this or was it too late? Had Mike already gotten so tired of her that there was no way back? Was he already in love with Carla? As her mind and thoughts were racing she almost didn't see the dog running across the street, she saw it just in time and steered the car in the other direction just in time to save the dog. What she didn't know was that she was about to crash into a pole.

In the Hospital

Mary didn't know how she got there; all she knew was that all of the bright lights shining in her face were too much. She tried to guard her face from the light, but it was too bright. A man in a white robe took her hand and held it and comforted her. "Everything's going to be okay, you're safe here," the voice calmingly said. The closer she looked at the man's face the more details she could see; she saw the long hair, the long white robe he was wearing. "Jesus?" she said. "Jesus, is that you?" she repeated. The doctor turned to her friend Laura whose face was full of worry and concern. "This is completely normal; she's still on heavy drugs. The accident could have been worse, she is lucky to be alive. Someone must have been watching over her," the doctor said. "Well thank God she's doing alright; and it was about time she found Jesus," Laura said feeling slightly relieved of the good news the doctor had told her. But even with the assuring tone of the doctor, she was still worried about her friend which was lying in the hospital bed. "Jesus is that you?" Mary continued mumbling. "Yes Jesus is here honey, he's here," Laura affirmed touching her friend's arm carefully. Laura had been trying to call Mike several times to let him know that his wife was in the hospital, but couldn't reach him. She went out in the hallway of the hospital, and tried to call Mike again. Laura was in the hallway trying to call Mike when the doctor called on her. Laura hurried back into the hospital room where Mary was lying and was starting to wake up even more. "What happened? Where am I? Where is Mike?" Mary said as she was trying to lift her head slowly. "Oh my head, it hurts," she said as she put her head back on the pillow. "You were in an accident. You were lucky. It could have been much worse," the doctor said to Mary while Laura was standing next to him with a worried face. "What? An accident? Where is Mike?" Mary said confused. "Mike is not here yet, I've been trying to call him. He hasn't answered yet," Laura said. Mary suddenly got stressed, remembering the messages she had seen. "He's with that woman; I know it. I have to go to him. I have to tell him I'm sorry, I have to save our marriage before he leaves me for her," Mary said stressed out while still in pain. "Mary," Laura said. "You don't understand how bad shape you're in right now. You need to rest and heal your body first, then you can try to save your marriage. But first you have to get well," Laura said. The doctor looked at Mary. "Recovering from this can take some time; it might take some time to train up your basic skills like walking, holding utensils to eat and things like that," the doctor said. "How am I going to save my marriage if I can barely walk and eat without help?" Mary said. "That's something we have to figure out," Laura said. "But now let's focus on your recovery and getting you well," Laura said and then excused herself to go out to the hallway to take a call.

Mike Gets the Call

Mike had gone out of Carla's office to take the call, but the phone had stopped ringing. He had tried to call back, but nobody answered. So he went back into Carla's office again, to finish the conversation. "You look so stressed out these days Mike; if there's anything I can do to make you feel better, just let me know," Carla said and looked straight at him. Then Mike's phone was calling again. He answered without leaving the room this time. He answered the phone and listened as Laura explained and told him about what had happened to Mary. "Mary you said? At the hospital? I'm coming right away," Mike said to Laura on the phone. He then turned to Carla. "I have to go, my wife needs me." He hurried out of the building to go to the hospital. He hurried to the hospital as Laura had told him that Mary was there after an accident. He couldn't help but to blame himself, maybe it was his actions that had caused her to be stressed and in some way had led to the accident. He got into the hospital entrance and explained who he was and who he was visiting. After waiting for a while, a nurse came and showed him the way to the room where Mary was. Mary was sleeping and she had a white bandage around her head and bruises in her face. She was alone in the room, as Laura had already left to pick up her children from school. The nurse had updated him on what had happened and how lucky Mary had been to survive, and how it could take months to train up her basic skills. He kissed Mary's forehead and sat down on a chair beside of her bed and held her hand tightly. He hadn't prayed in a long time and he figured that now was a good time to start praying again. He felt so bad about how he'd acted lately, their arguments, going out with Carla and all of the things that may had led to this moment they were in. "Forgive me God," Mike said quietly while looking up. He didn't know what more to say and couldn't find the right words to say, so he just continued to hold Mary's hand tightly.

Will Laura Stand by Her Man?

Laura had picked up the children from school and was at home cooking dinner for the family as her husband came home from work. "You're home early," Laura said cold, as it was rare he seemed to bother to come home in time for family dinner anymore. Her husband looked sad and depressed. "What's up with you?" Laura said as she was putting plates on the table. "I don't want to talk about it right now," he said as he sat down for family dinner. The children came down to the kitchen from their rooms to eat dinner also. They were all eating quietly until Laura broke the silence by telling what had happened that day to her best friend Mary. "She's in the hospital now, but the doctor says she will get well again and recover through months of training." Laura explained. "That's terrible mom," her oldest daughter Allison said. "I hope she recovers quickly," Allison said and then shook her head in disbelief and realised the same thing could happen to her own mother. "What if something happened to you? I don't want a new step-mother," Allison said. "Where did you get that from?" Laura said. "Some girls at school were teasing me, saying that dad is dating the mother of someone in school and that I would get her as my step-mother," Allison replied. Laura pretended to have a confused look on her face. "Where would they get that idea from?" Laura said as she gave James a certain look. Allison cried and went upstairs to her room. Shortly thereafter, James also walked away from the table and went upstairs. Laura cleaned up the kitchen after dinner and the two youngest children went to their rooms to do homework. When she was done with cleaning up, she went upstairs to take care of the laundry that was piling up. She went to the bedroom where James was lying and she started picking up clothes around the room and dropped it into the laundry box. "What is it with you today?" Laura said to James as she shook her head and picked up the laundry box and went to the laundry room. As she was doing laundry her husband James came in with a remorseful and depressed look. "Have I ruined it for us?" he said. "Ruined what?" she said carelessly continuing doing the batch of laundry that was in front of her. "Our marriage?" he said. "What happened to your other lady, was she busy today, since you're even bothering to be at home today?" Laura answered cold. "She left me," James said. "She found out about you and the children. She said she didn't want to be a homewrecker or a stepmother, so she ended the relationship. She's already found someone new." James looked down. "Well I can't say you didn't get what you deserved," Laura said. She walked out of the laundry room and left James behind. She walked back into the kitchen to make herself a cup of tea, getting ready to watch her favourite drama show on TV. She sat down in the living room with her cup of tea and homemade cookies. James had followed her around like a puppy, trying to get her attention, or some kind of reaction or sense about what she was thinking. After all these years together he thought he could read his wife as an open book, but this time he was clueless about what she was feeling. It seemed as if she had closed the book, and he was wondering if he would ever be in another chapter of her life. Or had he lost it all because of his mistakes, had he lost this wonderful life they had built up together and their wonderful children. He knew Laura was a beautiful woman and could get a new man just by blinking her long eye lashes and using that Southern charm that had caught him the first time they met. Just the thought of her with someone new was killing him, and the thought of her moving in with someone new and the children having a step-father. He couldn't stand it. He was starting to get desperate to get some kind of reaction from Laura. "Are you going to leave me?" he said. "I don't know," Laura said carelessly as she continued to watch the TV show.

Andrew Starts Dating Someone Else

Andrew had been convinced by his friends to go out with a girl they knew. They claimed that doing so could help him get Jennifer to see him differently. Andrew didn't know how he was feeling about it; he hadn't dated any girl since he had met Jennifer. He had always waited and hoped that she would eventually proclaim her love for him. He thought she would have done that a long time ago, but it never happened, so this was his last resort. He didn't understand how dating another woman could solve anything, but he had proclaimed his love for Jennifer and she had rejected him cold blooded. Maybe it was time for him to date other women anyway. He had wanted to be in a relationship for a long time now, he wanted to get married and have children in the near future. If Jennifer wasn't the one, then maybe he had to start trying to find someone else. Eric had introduced him to a single girl named Sheila. She was the opposite of Jennifer in every way. Jennifer had long brown beautiful hair, while Sheila had straight, blonde hair. Jennifer was an introvert and Sheila, was definitely an extrovert as she couldn't seem to stop talking. Where Jennifer was independent and not desperate for a relationship at all, Sheila seemed like she would do anything to be in a relationship. He had invited Sheila to come and meet him at the apartment first, and then they had planned to go out and eat at a restaurant later. He went down to meet her at the entrance of the apartment building, and then followed Sheila up to his and Jennifer's apartment. He entered the apartment with Sheila and they went to the kitchen and sat there talking. Not long after that, Jennifer came out of her room into the kitchen unaware and unsuspecting of Andrew's date being there. She went straight to the kitchen cabinets and was trying to find something as she continued talking to Andrew, still unaware of Sheila being in the room. Suddenly she heard Sheila giggle and turned around quickly, and was surprised and caught off guard by Andrew's visitor. "Oh, Hi," Jennifer said to

Sheila. "I didn't know Andrew was having visitors," Jennifer said with a look of surprise on her face. She was not only shocked to see Sheila whom she knew through her friends, but she had never experienced Andrew bringing other girls to their shared apartment at all. He barely invited his guy friends over, let alone any girls. She couldn't be mad at Sheila because first of all Jennifer wasn't in a relationship with Andrew, and second of all Sheila didn't know Andrew as they had never met before. Andrew saw the look on Jennifer's face. "Don't worry, we will be leaving soon. I just wanted to show Sheila where I live." "Ah, okay," Jennifer replied, being unsure about what she felt about the whole thing. The whole situation had made her feel something, but she wasn't exactly sure of what those feelings meant.

Learning to Walk Again

Mary was finally home again, after she had been several weeks in the hospital. She was training up her ability to walk, together with her physiotherapist who had come to their home. "Yeah that's it, one more step now Mary." The physiotherapist Gina said, as Mary was struggling to take one step after another. It was something that had been so easy before, something she was sad to have ever taken for granted. To walk, run and move without help, there was nothing she desired more than that now. Mary was starting to make more and more progress when it came to learning to walk again and learning to use utensils, but it was still a struggle. She knew this whole situation was difficult to handle for Mike and had put a lot of pressure on him. She wasn't sure if he could handle any more pressures or burdens than what he already had. What she was the most afraid of, was that all of that pressure would make him give up on their marriage and push him right back into the arms of Carla again. It wasn't exactly the ideal situation; needing her husband to help her with the basic things as walking, eating, getting dressed and combing her hair. It wasn't exactly the ideal recipe for saving a marriage and keeping him away from other beautiful women. Mike was helping her to change clothes after the physiotherapy session and these thoughts were continuously going through her head. "Are you tired of me?" she asked. "If you want to leave me I can understand it Mike, I truly do. This isn't what you signed up for, feeding and dressing your wife." Mary looked at Mike, hoping to get some kind of clue from his body language and facial expressions. "Of course I'm not tired of you," Mike predictably said. She knew that he would say that, but was it really true? In his mind, Mike was wondering the same. Later that night when Mary was sleeping upstairs in the bedroom, Mike went down to the living room and turned on the TV as he couldn't sleep. The television turned on to the sermon channel again, which was a channel Mary had been watching more and more often since the accident. The preacher T.D Jakes was speaking and talking about how he, after his wife's accident had to help her after she got severe injuries. *"I prayed for her, I took care of her, I cooked for her, I washed her hair. I taught her how to walk — literally. I stood in front of her and said, 'You can do this,' and taught her to walk again. It brought us together. We have an unexplainable connection... I guess, at the core, we're friends."* Mike sat in his own thoughts after the sermon and thought about what his wife had said, how this wasn't what he had signed up for, but isn't it in difficult times a husband is supposed to protect, provide and take extra good care of his wife? He looked through his phone, searching for Carla's phone number and was about to delete it. He should have deleted it and blocked it for a long time ago. He was about to press the delete button, but for some reason he wasn't able to do it and he put his phone down on the table, looking at the photo of Carla.

Is Jennifer Catching Feelings?

Jennifer was sitting in her own thoughts in the living room of her apartment. It had been several weeks now, since Andrew had started dating Sheila. Jennifer had been sure that Andrew couldn't survive a day with that woman as she knew how much Andrew hated excessive chattering and superficial things and conversations. Sheila seemed to be all those things she thought Andrew hated, but they were still hanging out and had done so often for weeks now. The more she saw them together, the more annoyed Jennifer was becoming. As an introvert, she generally disliked people invading her private space. Maybe that's all it was, or was it something more? She called her friend Sarah to chat. "Hey Jennifer," Sarah answered. "Just wait one second, I'm making dinner here," Sarah said as Jennifer could hear Sarah telling her chef to make an extra portion for a friend that was coming over to visit. "Making dinner huh?" Jennifer said sarcastically. "Well, it's almost the same thing as making dinner. It's my kitchen, my groceries, and I decide what's for dinner. How are you doing? It's been a while since I've heard from you. How is Andrew? Has he made any more proclamations of love lately?" Sarah said as she laughed lightly. "Well he has a new girl, Sheila of all people. It seems to be serious as they've been dating for weeks. I've never seen Andrew dating anyone, so it might be serious to him I guess," Jennifer said. "Wow Andrew dating Sheila. I didn't see that one coming. Well how do you feel about it?" Sarah asked, noticing Jennifer's slightly sad tone of voice. "I don't know. I don't think this living together as friends is working anymore. I'm thinking about asking him to move out," Jennifer said. Sarah was shocked. "After so many years together as friends? Jennifer it's clear that you like him more than you'd like to admit. You need to go and tell him how you feel, that you have feelings for him. Go get your man, girl!" Sarah said. "What is he even doing with that girl? She's nothing like his type," Jennifer said frustrated. "Why couldn't we just continue the way we were? We were good like that. If we try something more and it doesn't work out, then I will lose one of my best friends. I don't want that to happen," Jennifer said. Sarah sighed. "Well, a man can't wait forever Jennifer. Things can't always stay the same. Andrew proclaimed his love for you, and you rejected him and broke his heart. How do you think he's feeling? It's now or never Jennifer. You have to go and fight for your man or let him go and let him be happy with someone else. You can't keep him waiting in the friend zone for ever."

Mary Writes the Script

Mary had been working at a fashion magazine as a writer and had earned some recognition for her work there, but it had been writing scripts which had brought her the most success. It had helped her to be able to buy quite a nice apartment in Manhattan. The scripts she had been writing in the past were good, but she was sure that the one she was currently writing was even better. She had a good feeling about it. She had been training up her basic functions and was able to use her hands again. Her legs however, were a different story. The only advantage was that she now had a lot of time to sit down and write a new script. She was writing a romantic comedy which had been inspired by the dream she had, about men from Mars and women from Venus who were as different as they could be. She had been writing it for some time now, and was re-writing and perfecting her work of art. She laughed out loud at some of the scenes she had written and envisioned it playing on a big movie screen. While Mary was in the living room writing on her computer, Mike was downstairs in the man-cave. He was sitting on his brown leather couch, talking to his father Joe on the phone. "How is she doing?" Mike's father Joe asked through the phone. Mike sighed. "Well the recovery is moving forward, but the progress is slow. It's difficult," Mike answered. It had been several months now, since the accident. Mary had been working with a good physiotherapist and she'd been making some progress, but it hadn't been easy for either one of them. Before the accident Mary had been the one making the most money, now he was the main provider. He honestly didn't know if they would be able to keep their beautiful house on only his income which was not even close to what Mary had been making. "Your mother, she's praying for you both. She knows that you are going through difficult times. It's the difficult times that will either make or break a marriage. It's in the difficult times you'll figure out how strong your love and relationship really is.

You know that the vows say in both good and bad times. In the bad times you just have to fight a little bit harder to keep the love strong," Joe said. Mike sighed and hoped that he and Mary would be able to overcome all of the challenges they were experiencing.

Jennifer Confronts Andrew

Jennifer was just ending a conversation with Sarah as Andrew was entering the apartment. Sheila had followed him to the entrance and they were saying goodbye. "I have to hang up now Sarah," Jennifer said as she hung up the phone. Andrew said goodbye to Sheila and closed the door, he said a short "Hi" to Jennifer and went to the kitchen. He was making himself something to eat and was texting on the phone and smiling as if he was reading something he liked. "Hey, Andrew," Jennifer said as she was sitting down in the kitchen chair. "You and Sheila have been hanging out a lot lately. You really like her don't you?" Jennifer said as she looked at Andrew's facial expression when he answered. "Yeah, she's cool to hang around with. I like her yeah," Andrew answered. "You know Andrew, we've lived together for a long time as friends, but maybe the time has come to live our own two separate lives. I don't know if this living situation is working anymore. I think I need my own space. You know I don't really like having strangers in my private living space," Jennifer said. "Sheila is not a stranger and what do you mean with living our own separate lives?" Andrew replied as he was shocked by what Jennifer had just said. This is not what was supposed to happen. According to his friends, Jennifer would see him with Sheila and would want to be with him more. Andrew was starting to regret bringing Sheila into his life, even though he had actually started to like Sheila a bit. She wasn't as shallow as he had initially thought. He had thought that some company was better than being alone, but if this was the price to pay, then it wasn't worth it. He was still hoping that Jennifer would change her mind about him and would want something more than just a friendship. Jennifer interrupted his thoughts as she continued talking. "What are you even doing with that girl; she's not even your type. First of all she's blonde; since when were you into blondes? And she's so talkative, it's like she can't stop talking, blah, blah, blah this and that. How are you able to even put up with her? I don't get it." Jennifer sighed after getting her frustrations with Sheila out. "Woah, wait. What is this Jennifer? I've never heard you talk like this. Why are you talking about her that way? It almost sounds as if you're jealous. If it wasn't for the fact that I know you don't have any feelings for me, as you've made that very clear, then I would think that you were jealous. But if you don't have any feelings for me, then why are you acting this way?" As he was asking her, it suddenly dawned on him. Maybe she did have feelings for him? He looked at her as Jennifer was suddenly quiet and was looking down while avoiding his gaze. "Wait, do you have feelings for me?" Andrew said slightly confused. She walked out of the kitchen and to her room and closed the door.

Chapter 4

Will Laura Stand by Her Man?

Laura was sitting in her car and was on the way to her parents who were living in the South. It had been hard for her, to face her husband every day, to look him in the eyes and remember that he had been with someone else and was willing to destroy what they had built up all these years. She had been thinking about whether she should continue to stand by her husband, or if she should leave him. Her husband had made it clear that he regretted his behaviour, and he was painfully waiting for her decision. She wasn't going to make it easy for him and make him think that it was okay to do the same thing again. No she had let him wait, and then she let him wait some more. She didn't give out any clues; she took long weekends away with the girls at the spa and was enjoying her life, reminding him that she could easily enjoy a life without him. That's what she could do, if she wanted to and if she decided to. She had been doing this for months now. It seemed as if he had gotten the point by now and that the lesson had been learned, but before she made her decision, there was someone else she wanted to talk to. She remembered the Bible verse of Proverbs 15:22. *"Without counsel plans fail, but with many advisers they succeed."* She needed advice, before she was about to make one of the biggest decisions of her life. Laura had needed a break from her husband and had decided to go home to visit her family in the South for the weekend. She was hoping it could give her the clarity she needed to make a final decision about whether to leave her husband or continue to stay in the marriage. Would she be able to forgive him for the great betrayal and the hurt he had caused her? Right now she didn't know, as it was difficult enough just to look at him and be in the same house as him. Thinking about him didn't exactly give her butterflies in her stomach, but rather nausea which made her want to throw up. She had arrived at her parents' house, which also was her childhood home as her parents had never moved from there. She took a look at the large two story white colonial house with large brown entrance doors and golden door knobs. She looked at the large garden and the water fountain in the middle. She admired the perfectly well attended flower beds that were in front of the house. It was good to be home she thought to herself. She took her golden suitcase and rolled it over the entrance door sill. Her large, expensive, leather purse was hanging over her shoulder. "Hello. Mom? Dad? I'm here." It didn't take long before both of her parent's came and welcomed her with a warm loving hug. The smell of Southern comfort food was filling the house. "That smells so good Mom and I'm so hungry." Laura was looking forward to being spoiled with homemade comfort foods for a whole weekend. She hugged her mom and dad and went upstairs to the guest room and placed her bag and suitcase there. The current guest room used to be her room when she was younger. It used to be pink, but her parents had renovated it after she moved out. It was now white with nothing but a large dresser made of dark wood and a matching king sized bed. The only item still left in the room was a teddy bear with a pink dress, which had been her favourite item up until her teenage years. She looked at it and reminisced a happy childhood filled with wonderful memories and said a silent, "Thank you" to God as she remembered how blessed she had been. She knew that she was still blessed, despite what was going on between her and her husband. Her mom called her name from downstairs as dinner was ready. Laura took a quick look in the mirror and went downstairs to eat dinner with her parents. Her parents didn't really know much about what had happened between Laura and her husband. Laura already knew what they would think she should do with her marriage. For her parents, the promise of 'for better, for worse, in sickness and in health and until death do us part' was a promise made to God. It was a promise that should be kept, no matter what a married couple might feel or go through. Laura took a bite of her mom's heavenly Mac'n Cheese and the nostalgia and the memories of an easier time increased with every bite. The Peach Cobbler that was for dessert brought back even more memories of her childhood. Why did she have to go through this with her husband? Why couldn't God make them have the same stable and happy marriage which her parents and grandparents seemed to have had? Feeling the sting of bitterness, she tried to remember to be grateful and to focus on her blessings. "So how is Allison doing?" her mother Jill asked after she had taken a sip of the red wine she had in her glass. "She's doing great. She made it to the cheerleading team and she really loves it. She's been practicing a lot these days. I think it's good. It keeps her occupied and distracts her from getting into trouble. You know how teenagers are; if you don't keep them occupied they might do foolish things," Laura replied. "Yeah I remember how you were Laura, when you were in that age," her father Charles said. "I wasn't that bad, dad." Laura rolled her eyes as she remembered her teenage years. She had been pretty good at school. She had always been a people pleaser who wanted those around her to be happy, but she also remembered some of the foolish mistakes she had made. It was good that her parents didn't know everything that had happened. After dinner Laura went upstairs and took a nap on the bed in the guest room as she needed to recharge her energy. She needed some extra energy to go out with some of her friends later. Later that night Laura and some of her friends from high school went to the local bar, to have a few drinks and have a girl's night out. Laura had been out until late into the morning hours, way later than what she had planned and long after the hours her parents thought would be a proper time to come home. Thankfully she was a grown woman. Her parent's might punish her with guilt and shame, but they couldn't ground her anymore if she didn't arrive before midnight. The reason she had stayed out so late is that when the girls were ready to leave and were on their way out of the bar, Laura ran into an old crush, whom she hadn't seen in a long time. "What are you doing here Laura? I thought you were in New York living the big city life?" He had said. "Luke? Is that you? I haven't seen you since high school. My, oh my; how you've grown since then." Laura had said looking up at the man who now had a face full of beard and who had grown a few more muscles since the last time she had seen him. He had convinced her to stay and talk for a while, which she did. "A while" turned into hours, and she was having way more fun than she should have. Luke had made her laugh and made her enjoy his company so much that it had been difficult to leave. Luke seemed to enjoy spending time with her too; a little too much it seemed as he suddenly kissed her." Laura froze as she'd realized she shouldn't have been there in the first place. She'd realized that spending time with another man like that, almost made her as bad as her husband. She could understand how one thing could lead to another and how mistakes could be made. Her husband was as human and vulnerable as she had been that night. Laura had quickly excused herself and told Luke that she needed to go. On the way home she had cried. The tears stemmed from all of the frustration, bitterness and regret she currently felt. Thankfully her parents were sleeping when she arrived at the house. She went upstairs to the guestroom and dropped down on the bed, she was still crying. She did something she hadn't done in a long time; she took her brown teddy bear and held it close to her. She felt silly, but the childhood item brought some comfort to the inner turmoil she was experiencing. Shortly after that she fell asleep.

Andrew Moves Out

Jennifer didn't know why it was so difficult for her to admit and reveal her feelings for Andrew. She was still scared that opening up to Andrew would ruin her friendship with him. They had lived together as friends for a long time, but there were many things he didn't know about her. There were many things they hadn't talked about, especially things that had to do with love and relationships. He didn't know that she was celibate and was saving herself for marriage. He didn't know that she wanted to raise her children in her own Jewish religion. Neither did he really know that her parents would never accept the thought of her marrying someone who was not Jewish or a "goy" as they called it. She had been told countless stories about how relationships between Jews and non-Jews and interfaith marriages didn't work out. As a non-Jew, there were so many things he just wouldn't be able to understand. After the conversation they'd had in the kitchen the other day, she had gone to her room and thought about these things. After much thought and consideration she had decided that the best thing was if they moved from each other, and that anything else would just complicate things. Andrew was packing his things into boxes and carrying yet another box of things to the hallway as she was just standing there watching him, trying to decode his facial expressions and body language. "I think that's the last box. I will just take another look around to be sure I've packed up everything," Andrew said as he was about to go to his room. "Don't go," Jennifer said suddenly as she grabbed his arm, and was a bit surprised by her own reaction. "What do you mean, don't go?" he said confused. "I'm literally packing up the last box here, and now you're saying. Don't go? I'm about to move out Jennifer, if you have anything you want to say to me, you should say it now," Andrew said with a look of frustration. "I can't wait for ever Jennifer," he said and looked at her, waiting for a response. As she didn't say anything more, because she was trying to hold the tears back, he went to his room to see if he had packed everything. The room was empty, the room he had spent so many years in. So many years and so many memories, and now it was all ending. He was almost about to get emotional, but couldn't let himself. It was almost as if his father was standing on his shoulder whispering in his ear. *"Real men don't cry and show emotions Andrew."* He held back the tears, straightened up and went back out towards the hallway and walked past Jennifer who was still standing there watching him. As he was about to say goodbye and walk out the door she came up to him and hugged him. They had given each other friendly hugs before, but this time it seemed different. It was as if she didn't want him to let her go, so he didn't. They hugged for a long time. Eventually their embrace was interrupted by Andrew's friend Eric who came to help him move the boxes into the moving van they had rented.

Andrew and Eric were walking towards the moving van with the last two boxes, his friend Eric apologized. "Apologize for what?" Andrew said. "It was my suggestion to try to make her jealous. I didn't know it would come to this, after you've been living together for so many years. It worked for me, but unfortunately it didn't work the same way for you. So I'm sorry," Eric said. "No problem, you were just trying to help, you couldn't have known that this would happen," Andrew said. "Well at least you have Sheila," Eric said. "Well not exactly. I'm going to end our relationship. It wasn't right to use her like that, while I was still in love with another woman. She deserves better than that. I need a break and I need to try to figure out what to do with my life. I've been working on this new app, which might help me earn a lot of money. There's this company that seems to be interested in investing in it, but I don't know yet. I just need to figure things out and get used to this new situation." As they were driving in the car, they were both silent. Andrew was sitting in his own thoughts while he was listening to the song 'Hallelujah' that was on the radio. He listened to the lyrics. *"All I ever learned from love, was to shoot at someone who outdrew you. It's no complaint that you ear tonight, it's no pilgrim who's seen the light. It's a cold and it's broken Hallelujah..."* It was so surreal, that he wasn't living with Jennifer anymore, after so many years together. The plan to make her his girl had gone terribly wrong; this wasn't what was supposed to happen. He could feel the weight of the depressing thoughts he was thinking. He didn't know if things could ever change for the better after messing it up so badly. The only thing that gave him hope and comfort, was the memory of the last embrace between him and Jennifer. As they arrived at Andrew's new place they got out of the car and started walking towards the place where Andrew was going to stay. "Well I hope you like our basement," Eric said. "Now, here are the rules. Rule number one: No loud music after 10 o'clock okay? Number two: I want rent to be in before the end of the month or I'll kick you out," Eric said joking with Andrew who would now live in his basement for a while.

Laura's Humble Realisation

Laura arrived back home at her house with a greater sense of peace, but also with a greater sense of humility because of realizing that she too could also make mistakes. Her husband wasn't perfect and neither was she. The only way they could make things work, and have the kind of long lasting marriage which Laura desired, was through forgiving each other's mistakes and through working things out. Laura realized that there was no such thing as a perfect marriage, and her parents and grandparents had probably gone through their fair share of struggles behind the scenes. Maybe she had an unrealistic expectation of how a marriage should be, because other people's marriages seemed to look so perfect on the outside. She expected marriage to be like a romantic comedy, with lots of fun and romance. She needed to have more realistic expectations of what love and marriage really was, if this was going to work out. Her husband greeted her at the door with a look that told her that he had truly missed her. He didn't know if he could hug her or not, as she had been cold towards him for months now. Laura didn't want to hug him, as it felt as if she was rewarding him for his bad behaviour. But she couldn't help it; she had missed him more than she had wanted and her body moved closer to him and embraced him. She cried a few tears and he comforted her. Laura realized how much she had missed her husband. Not only during the weekend, but after all of those months giving him a cold shoulder, it was so good to feel his embrace again.

A Walk to Remember

Mary's phone rang and interrupted her in the middle of writing her script. It was Jennifer. "Hey Jennifer. How are you?" Mary said in the phone, trying to multitask by talking and writing the script at the same time. "He has moved out," Jennifer said with a sad tone. "Who has moved out?" Mary asked. "Andrew," Jennifer answered. "Andrew has moved out? Why? Didn't you tell him that you have feelings for him too?" Mary said. "No I just froze and couldn't do it. But the way he hugged me before he left... we've never hugged like that before. It was... it made me feel... I think I'm in love with him Mary, I think I have to let him know," Jennifer said kind of relieved by getting things out in the open. She hoped it would be easier to say it to Andrew now after she had said it openly to someone else. "You have to tell him Jennifer, before time runs out. Andrew is a handsome guy, he might find someone else and then it will be too late," Mary said. "You're right Mary, I have to tell him. I will tell him at the party at Sarah's place tonight," Jennifer said, hoping she would find the courage to actually do so. Not long after Mary had hung up the phone and ended the conversation, her physiotherapist Gina arrived and they started doing the same exercises they had been doing for months now. Mary had progressed from using a wheel chair, to crutches. Today she was going to try to walk without the crutches also. The last time she had tried, she had almost been able to walk without the crutches. "Yeah that's it; one more step now Mary," Gina said, as Mary was walking and taking one step after another. "You can do it," Gina said encouraging Mary as she was becoming better and better. After a few rounds back and forth she finally did it, she was finally able to walk without the crutches. "I did it! I can walk again," Mary said happy. She said a silent, "Thank you" to God and felt a few tears coming down her cheeks. For the first time in a long time she was crying happy tears.

Party at Sarah's Place

Jennifer arrived at Sarah's place and the party was already in full force. She was not a fan of parties, but she knew Andrew was currently and temporarily living in Sarah and Eric's basement and she wanted an excuse to get close to him. After their last embrace that day when he had moved out, she had found herself thinking about him more and more. She found it increasingly difficult to not think about him. She knew she shouldn't have these thoughts and feelings for a non-Jew, as her parents had told her to marry within her own religion. Despite this, she just knew she had to see him and talk to him. Jennifer walked in through the entrance door and saw a crowd of strangers. She searched for a familiar face in the crowd and went to the kitchen where she knew Sarah would be bossing the chefs around, as she often did. "There you are!" Sarah said when she saw Jennifer and hugged her. "How nice to finally see you at a party, you don't have any hidden agendas for coming or what?" Sarah said and joked since she already knew Jennifer was there because she wanted to see Andrew. "Of course I know why you're here; you're not here for the party, you're here for Andrew. Do you want me to show you where he is?" Sarah said. "Yes if you could, that would be great," Jennifer said slightly embarrassed as Sarah could see right through her intentions. They walked across the hallway and then down the stairs which led to the basement, and the room where Andrew was at. "I will let you do your thing and go get your man. I will go upstairs and entertain the guests," Sarah said as she smiled and walked back up the stairs. Jennifer knocked on Andrew's door and waited for him to open. Andrew opened the door, thinking it was his friend Eric. "I'm coming soon Eric," he said as he opened the door. He was surprised when he saw that it wasn't Eric, but Jennifer. "Jennifer? What are you doing here?" he said surprised as he closed the door behind him. "Andrew, I have something I need to tell you," Jennifer said. Jennifer wanted to say it quickly and right away before she lost the courage to do so. "What? Has something happened? Are you okay?" Andrew asked. "Yes I'm okay. It's just that I've had a lot of time to think and I don't know how to say this but... I really miss you," she said. "Miss me?" he said. "Andrew, I have feelings for you, I....I'm in love with you," Jennifer said with a sigh of relief, finally able to reveal the things she had been keeping inside. Andrew felt a mix of joy and confusion and didn't quite know what to say. "I... wasn't expecting this today. I would love to invite you in but I'm kind of busy, I have a visitor," he said. Jennifer was a bit caught off guard by his response, as she had been imagining a different scenario in her mind. "Oh, okay. I'm sorry. I should just go then," Jennifer said and was about to go, when Andrew grabbed her arm. "Don't go. I will tell her to leave. It's just that I thought you were..." Jennifer stopped him in his sentence. "It's a girl?" she asked. Just right then Andrew's door opened and a girl talked to him. "Are you coming Andrew?" Jennifer looked at Andrew and the girl, and just wanted to get out of there. "I shouldn't have come. Go back to your girl Andrew. I will go," Jennifer said and then she walked away and back up the stairs through the crowd of people and went back home. Later that night after the party Andrew was sitting in the kitchen talking with Sarah. He had told her about what had happened with Jennifer. "Then when Jennifer saw her, she misunderstood the situation and ran off. I didn't get time to tell her," Andrew explained. "You guys just need to get married soon, before you mess things up anymore. You already know each other and you've already been best friends like for ever. There's no reason to wait. Ask her out and give her a ring or something, and start a wonderful life together. She's already saving herself for marriage, so you better give her a ring fast, before you both do something stupid," Sarah said. "What, she's saving herself for marriage? She's never told me that," Andrew said. "Oh... I assumed you knew, since you've known her and lived with her for such a long time," Sarah said realizing that she had unintentionally revealed Jennifer's secret. "That's not important; I've already survived being in the friend zone for a really long time. If I can handle that, then I can handle anything. I would need your help though. I want to plan something special for her," Andrew said pleased as he was realizing that it was finally happening. Jennifer was finally starting to open up to him.

Andrew Visits Jennifer

Andrew knew he had to talk to Jennifer and clear up the misunderstanding that had happened at the party. The moment he had been waiting for since he'd met Jennifer in college had finally happened, but what could have been such a beautiful moment had been messed up by a misunderstanding. Andrew knew he had to talk to Jennifer and clear things up before she closed off her feelings completely and was scared to open up to him again. He wasn't sure what her reaction would be when he knocked on her door, but he felt like he had nothing to lose and everything to gain to try. He knocked at her door and waited, but nobody opened. He knocked again and waited some more but still nobody opened up. Suddenly the door opened up and a Jewish looking man opened the door. "Can I help you? Are you here to visit Jennifer?" the guy said. "Yes, but if it's inconvenient I can come back later," Andrew said not sure how to react or what to say. He had never really experienced Jennifer having visitors all of the years they lived together, so he was a bit surprised and caught off guard. "No, just come on in. She's just in the shower, she will be finished soon. Come in and join us," the guy said. "Us?" Andrew said confused. "Yes her parents are here also. My name is Reuben, by the way," he said while making a gesture as to tell Andrew to come in. Andrew, unsure about what to do, reluctantly entered the apartment that led straight to the white spacious living room with lots of green plants. Jennifer's parents were sitting on the couch. They were looking at him with scepticism as if they were wondering about what he was doing there. Andrew looked around to see if he could see Jennifer, but could not see her anywhere. He could hear the shower from the bathroom down the hallway next to his former bedroom. He wasn't sure if he should sit down or not, and pointed to the bathroom where Jennifer was. "Is she finished soon? Should I....." Jennifer's father interrupted Andrew. "Sit down now, she will come soon. Aren't you going to introduce yourself?" Andrew had lived a long time with Jennifer, but had never gotten to meet her parents. She always made it a point to never introduce her male friends to her parents as they were very strict and religious. She usually went to their place to visit and the few times they had visited her it had been when Andrew had been out of the house. They didn't know that one of the rooms in the house had been his former bedroom, as Jennifer had always closed it, excusing it as being too messy to be shown to them. Something which was partially true as Andrew wasn't the most organized guy out there. It had been mostly Jennifer who had kept the apartment neat, clean and organized, something which she seemed to love as she never really complained about it. She always seemed happy when she was doing domestic things, putting on music and almost dancing around as she was happily doing chores most people seemed to hate. Andrew came to remember all of the things he loved about her as his thoughts were interrupted by her father Abraham who again repeated the question. "Aren't you going to introduce yourself young man?" Abraham's strict and firm tone made Andrew more than just slightly uncomfortable. "Yes sir, eh... I'm Andrew; a friend of Jennifer." Andrew was feeling awkward and insecure as he could feel the judgmental look of her father, who was scanning him up and down to try to figure out what kind of guy he was. "Jennifer has a male friend? Since when could a man and woman be just friends?" Abraham looked at Jennifer's mother when he said it. Thankfully for Andrew, Jennifer was finished with showering and came out of the bathroom. Caught off guard and not able to hide being surprised she said, "Andrew! What are you doing here?" As the parents were wondering about the same thing they were following their conversation and body language. "I'm... I was just, I was about to leave, but your friend, he opened the door and then I...." He stuttered as he was being nervous about Jennifer's parents, especially her father who didn't seem too impressed with him. "Come here Andrew. I have something to show you," Jennifer said in an attempt to save him from her parents and his awkward rambling. Andrew was relieved and went to the other end of the apartment with Jennifer dragging him there. When they were in a place where they were sure Jennifer's parents couldn't see or hear them, then they started talking. "Jennifer, I'm so sorry. I didn't know your parents were here. I really messed things up. I should have just gone home right away when that guy opened up the door," Andrew said feeling guilty for doing anything that could give her problems or make her feel bad. "They came earlier than I expected, that's why I was in the shower and…" Jennifer was interrupted by Andrew. "Jennifer, that girl, the other day at my place, it wasn't what it seemed like. She's just a family member of Sarah and…" Jennifer stopped him in the middle of the sentence. "It's okay Andrew, I know. Sarah called me and told me everything. That girl was her cousin and you were teaching her how to play the guitar." Despite Jennifer's calm and assuring tone, Andrew still felt bad about what had happened. "I'm sorry if it made you feel bad, it wasn't how I wanted it to happen. I've been waiting for you to say those words to me for such a long time. I'm here now, if you want to say it again?" Andrew said. "Andrew, I still feel the same way, but I don't think this is the right moment. I have visitors and they are waiting." When Jennifer said that, he was reminded of the guy that was visiting her together with her parents. "By the way, who was that guy in the living room? Is it your friend or a family member or something?" he said slightly jealous and afraid that it was a date or something more than just a relative. The last thing he needed in his attempt to make her his, was another man. "Actually it's someone my parents brought here…" Jennifer said as she was looking down seemingly trying to avoid looking in Andrew's eyes. "So it's a family friend?" Andrew said trying to get answers. "My parents are thinking that it's time for me to get married, so they are trying to set me up with this Jewish guy. They think he's perfect for me as he's in the same religion. He's got a good job, he goes to the Shul... I mean, the Synagogue every Sabbath and...." Andrew stopped her in her sentence. This was not what he wanted to hear. "What do you think Jennifer? Do you think he's perfect for you?" Andrew said trying to look for clues in her face as she was answering. As she was answering it was as if she was also trying to convince herself of all of the things her parents had told her about Reuben. "Well he's a really great guy, he's kind, he's considerate and he's Jewish like me. He reads the Torah every day, he understands my religion and culture and he bought me these flowers...." she said and pointed to a large bouquet of roses that was in a vase on the small wooden table in the hallway. The large golden mirror in front of the vase made it look twice as big. "So does this mean you're considering anything with this guy?" Andrew said hoping she would say no. "I don't know what to do Andrew... I mean, I know what I want, but I don't know what to do," she said now looking at him straight. "What do you want Jennifer? I wasn't asking what your parents want, I know what they want. What do you want?" Andrew said getting more desperate for a straight, honest and direct answer from Jennifer. "I want you Andrew, but the thing is, it's complicated. I'm complicated. I'm Jewish, you're not. I know my parents won't accept you. I want to raise my children in my religion, and it's something that's difficult to do for an..." She paused slightly as to find the right words. And I'm saving myself for..." Andrew interrupted her. "You're saving yourself for marriage. I know, Sarah told me. Jennifer, I'm willing to wait for you, I've been waiting for you since forever, and I'm willing to wait longer if necessary. You're everything I want, I don't want anybody else. So what if it's complicated? Nothing worth having is easy. I'm willing to be complicated together, with you," he said as he was looking straight at her. "That's why I wanted to invited you to dinner with me, next week. Will you?" Andrew looked at Jennifer, hoping she would say yes. "Jennifer? Her father was calling her name from the living room. "Are you coming? We're waiting for you here," her father Abraham said with the same strict and firm tone. "Yes, I'm coming." Jennifer looked at Andrew for a moment before she hugged him the same way she had done that day he had moved out, as if she didn't want to let go. She kept holding him until she realized she had to let go and go to her guests. "I have to go okay? I will call you; I will follow you to the door." Jennifer made a gesture that told Andrew to follow her. She followed him to the entrance door and said, "Well thank you Andrew for visiting, it was very nice to see you. See you another time. Bye." She said it in an overly friendly tone, as if she was trying to convince her parents that he was nothing more than just a friend.

Just Say Yes

Andrew had planned the whole thing, with a little help, okay a lot of help from Sarah. He wasn't good with this romance thing, so he was grateful for Sarah's help. After that day at Jennifer's apartment he had come home with mixed feelings. They had experienced such emotional moments together that day. Andrew was feeling as if he had made progress and was finally getting Jennifer to open up to him and let her guard down, but at the same time he was unsure whether she was considering her parents' opinions and suggestions. That's what was worrying him the most. Jennifer had finally agreed with going out to a restaurant with him. She had called him on the phone after her parents had left that day, she didn't have much time to talk so he didn't get the chance to ask her about that Reuben guy. Andrew sat down at the restaurant with Jennifer. She looked so beautiful, and he almost couldn't believe that he was lucky enough to be there with her. "You look so beautiful," he said and loved the fact that he could now say it to her straight. He could tell her what he really felt as she now knew about his true feelings for her. "So how did it go with your parents that day and that guy, what was his name?" Andrew said. "Reuben. That was his name. My parents went home a few hours after you left," Jennifer said as she took a sip of her water. "What about Reuben? Did he leave?" Andrew said almost holding his breath as he was waiting for her answer. "Yes he left together with them," Jennifer said as she saw the relieved look on Andrew's face. "Have you been thinking more about us?" Andrew said trying to figure out where they were standing in their relationship. "I've had a lot of time to think Andrew. I really have been thinking a lot... about us." Andrew was sensing some hesitation in her voice, and he interrupted her to stop her from saying something he didn't want to hear. "Jennifer, I know what kind of doubts you are having, so let me be clear. Whatever religion you want me to convert to; I will do it for you. I can be the guy your parents want me to be. Whatever you need me to do, I will do it for you. I even bought you these flowers," Andrew said and gave Jennifer her favourite flowers; pink roses. Jennifer looked at the flowers while smiling as she saw how beautiful they were. "They're beautiful Andrew. Thank you," she said. Andrew was nervous about what he was about to do next. He had already broken most of Eric's dating rules by letting Jennifer know that he'd basically do anything to be with her. He was almost starting to regret what he was about to do next. What if Sarah was wrong? Maybe it was too soon to ask her to marry him, even though they had been friends for a long time, and even though Jennifer was starting to have feelings for him. Maybe he should give her some more time to develop feelings for him? But what if he didn't ask her and Reuben did it before him?" If he didn't ask her right here and now, then he might regret it. Andrew made up his mind to continue with the plan. "I also want to ask you one thing," Andrew said. "What is that?" Jennifer asked. "Will you marry me and be my wife?" He asked. He pulled out the ring Sarah had helped him to pick out and brought it out of his pocket. He opened the box and showed Jennifer the ring. Jennifer looked at it with amazement and Andrew could tell that she liked the ring and thought it was beautiful. "I know you might think it's too soon, even though we've been friends for a long time. But I want you to know that I'm willing to take this next step with you if that's what you want." Jennifer seemed a bit shocked, but she didn't look like she was completely opposed to the idea. Andrew took the ring out of the box and put it on her finger. She looked at it and was amazed at the beauty of the ring. She couldn't stop looking at it. "Andrew, it's beautiful. I don't know what to say." Jennifer was staring at the ring with amazement. "Say yes," Andrew said with a hopeful look.

Chapter 5

Mike and Mary's Weekend in the South
Mike was sitting in the basement with his best friend Thomas and they were playing video games. They had been playing until long past midnight. Mary was upstairs in the bedroom looking at the clock, wondering if Mike would soon say goodbye to their guest and come and go to bed. She had been patient and had waited until after midnight, but Mike was still playing video games with his friend. Mary thought that it was time for their guest to go home, as they had to get up early in the morning to drive the long way to Mike's parents in the South. Mary had rolled up her hair with her pink rollers and was wearing her pink robe and pink slippers. She went down to the basement and saw the two guys acting like two young school boys as they were playing video games. They didn't even notice her at first until she purposefully cleared her throat. The guys' attention turned to her. They both looked at her and wondered what she wanted. "Mike, honey, don't you think that it's time to say goodbye to our guest and come to bed? Don't you remember that we're travelling to your parents in the morning? It's already past midnight." Mike didn't know that they had played video games for so many hours. Mike looked at his watch and then looked at Thomas. "Well the wife is right, I should go to bed and get some rest before we're travelling tomorrow." Mike then turned to Mary. "I will just follow Thomas to the door and I'll come to bed." Mary went upstairs while Mike followed Thomas to the door. "Wow, Mary, she looked different." Thomas commented. Thomas was used to seeing Mary all dolled up. He hadn't seen her without make-up and with hair rollers. "Yeah at bedtime she transforms into looking like another woman." Mike laughed. After they had chatted for a while, Mike then said goodbye to Thomas, closed the door and went upstairs to get some sleep.

The next morning, Mike and Mary were driving down the country roads towards Mike's parents' house. They were visiting his parents for the weekend, taking a break from the hectic New York City life. The music was playing on the radio as Mike was wearing his cowboy hat and singing along. "She likes a small town boy like me... she's my laid back in the front seat..." "I can be country too," Mary said jokingly as she took Mike's cowboy hat and put it on her own head. It was Mike's mother Susan who had suggested that they should come there for the weekend. She thought it would be good for their marriage, as she knew that Mike and Mary had been struggling. She was also hoping to feed her son some proper Southern food, knowing from conversations with her son that Mary didn't cook him proper homemade food. She was hoping to teach Mary to cook some of Mike's favourite Southern Comfort dishes. As Mike and Mary were continuing to drive down the road, another country song came on the radio and Mary looked at Mike. "Why do you love country music so much? That's old people's music," Mary said. Mary always thought it was funny teasing Mike about his weird taste in music. "Hey don't mock my music; this is the kind of music I grew up with. So yes maybe I'm a bit nostalgic, but I had a good childhood and that music brings me many good memories," Mike said. "I just don't get it. It's boring music to me," Mary said as she looked out of the window that was halfway open, and as her dark brown hair was blowing in the wind. She put her hand out of the window, feeling the freedom of driving on a country road with nothing but green trees and fields of barley on both sides of the car. She looked at Mike, how carefree and happy he looked as he was driving closer to his childhood home. She could see how content he was and wondered if he had been happier if they had lived in the country side, instead of the city. She imagined in her own mind how things would be if they had made different choices, if they had chosen to settle for a quiet life in the country side. She imagined them having a small house close to the river where Mike could go fishing and where he was teaching their son how to fish, if they had children. How she was indoors wearing an apron cooking and baking, with their daughter eagerly watching her every move, trying to learn how to be a good homemaker, for her own future husband. Mike interrupted her thoughts. "What were you thinking about? It's like you were in a different world there," he said. "Maybe I was," she answered, slightly sad to have been interrupted in the middle of her daydreaming. She was no stranger to daydreaming, but this kind of felt different, it felt more like maybe some kind of longing? They didn't have any children yet, but she could see the vision so clearly in her mind and she secretly wondered when it would happen for them. When would they get children? Mike was slowing down the car as he came to a crossroad that led to a smaller dirt road. "We're almost at my parents' house now," he said. "Wow your parents really do live in the middle of the woods," Mary said as they were driving deeper and deeper into what felt like an endless jungle, just instead of exotic trees there were lots of oak and pine trees. They eventually arrived to a large farm surrounded with large white fences. Mike parked the car and they both got out. His parents had moved back to his childhood home after Mike had graduated from college and moved out. His conservative, old fashioned parents figured out that the hectic liberal, modern city life wasn't anything for them. They had a different type of serenity, peace and sense of being content when they were in the country side. Mary, who had never visited them after they had moved there, understood that Mike hadn't made an understatement when he said that they lived deep into the woods and far out in the country side. She also realized that her high heels weren't the best choice for this trip as she was struggling with walking on the grass without getting her heels stuck in the ground. "I hope you brought some flats," Mike said as he saw how she was struggling. She wished that she had brought some flats too she realized, as she struggled her way to the front door where Mike's parents Joe and Susan were welcoming them. Mike and Mary entered the house and the smell of Southern food filled the house. Mike's mother Susan had made Mike's favourite homemade Southern comfort food and the table was covered with mac and cheese, meatloaf, potatoes, gravy and greens. Mike looked like he was in heaven, so did his mother being happy to see her son eat proper food. She looked at Mary. "Mike loves this food so much; I made it all the time when he and his siblings were younger. Mike told me you don't cook this kind of food. You know I can teach you how to make it if you want." Mary looked at Mike with certain look, which made him know that she wasn't too happy with Mike telling his mother that she couldn't cook. She then looked back at Susan. "Thank you Mrs. Matthews, but..." She was about to turn down the offer, but changed her mind. She remembered the talks she'd had with the marriage counsellor about how to improve their marriage. "Sure, I'd love to Susan." She answered instead. Mike seemed pleased as anytime he had tried to make his wife be domestic at anything he had failed. He felt like they were making some kind of progress with Mary being willing to compromise her usual unwillingness to be domestic.

Andrew Discovers His Roots

Andrew knew that Jennifer's parents wouldn't accept her marrying someone who wasn't a Jew, and Jennifer's choice would definitely be influenced by her parent's wishes. Andrew hoped and knew there was a chance that Jennifer would defy her parent's wishes and say yes to his proposal. The last time he had been with Jennifer, he had proposed to her. She said that she needed some more time to think, before she could give him an answer. If she were to say yes then he knew that he had to learn more about her religion, because she had made it clear that she wanted to raise her future children in her religion. He knew that learning more about her religion would bring them closer. Andrew went to the library to find books on the subject. He looked through books that had to do with Jewish religion and found two books which he found interesting. He found one book on interfaith marriages and another about people who had discovered their Jewish ancestry. He then took the books home and started reading. In one of the books, he read stories about people who had discovered that they had Jewish roots and ancestry. Some of them had discovered it through a DNA test. Andrew found the thought of that interesting. What if he had Jewish ancestry? Would that change Jennifer's parent's view of him? Would that make them more accepting of him and eventually influence Jennifer's decision to marry him? A few weeks later, Andrew had eventually decided to take a DNA test to find out more about his ancestry. When he had finally received the test results in the mail, he had teared open the large envelope and had been feeling a mix of excitement and nervousness about what the documents would reveal. He felt like that document could change everything. He had slowly pulled out the documents out of the envelope and took deep breath before he looked at the results. When he finally dared to look at the results, he almost couldn't believe it. This would change everything.

Sweet Country Life

Mike's mom Susan seemed as if she was in heaven when she was finally able to teach her son's wife how to cook. It was as if she thought her sons survival counted on Mary's ability to cook. "So here is my recipe for sweet tea. Now let me show you the recipe for Mike's favourite apple pie," Susan said as she was eagerly running around the kitchen finding the right ingredients. Mike came into the kitchen seeing his two favourite women dressed in aprons while they were cooking, baking and getting along. He inhaled the smell of the delicious apple pie, and he felt like he didn't ever want to leave the place. Maybe Mary could be domestic after all? The girl who barely knew how to open an oven? When they first moved in together he even had to help her with the child lock on the oven, that's how bad it was. Now here they were and she was learning to make his favourite food. There was also another benefit of being there, since Mike's mother was there cleaning up, Mary wasn't nagging him about not cleaning up his clothes either. He could get used to this. He was enjoying the view of the two women being busy cooking up delicious meals in the kitchen. He watched them for a moment before he interrupted them. "Me and dad are going out fishing," he said to them. "Alright then, go and catch something we can use for dinner tomorrow," Susan said to the two men as they went outdoors to the river that was nearby. Mike and his dad Joe took the fishing pole, hooked the bait and threw it out into the river. They were chatting as they were waiting to catch something they could use for dinner. "So how are you and Mary? You two seem to be in a good place," Joe said to Mike. "Well, we have been since we came here. It's something about getting away from it all, from the everyday life stress and the big city life, that changes things. This is exactly what we needed," Mike said as he was enjoying the summer breeze touching his skin in the middle of the warming sun. As the two men were chatting they could hear Mary talking from behind them as she was trying to come and join them, while struggling walking with her high heels shoes. "Doesn't she have any other shoes?" Mike's father said as he was watching her struggle. She eventually took off the high heel shoes, held the shoes in her hand and walked barefoot towards them. "Hey guys. Can I join you?" Mary said as she was coming closer. "Sure," Mike said. She sat down beside the two men as she inhaled the fresh country air. She looked around and saw how the wind was slowly moving the leaves on the trees. "It's actually kind of nice here," she said as she was surprised by liking anything else than the big city she loved so much. She considered herself a city girl, a New Yorker and proud of it, but she was kind of starting to like this place. "Can I try?" she said as she pointed towards the fishing pole. "What? You want to try fishing?" Mike said hesitating as he knew how his wife was. "I've never tried fishing, but I would like to try," she answered. "Well if you think you can do it, why not?" Mike said and handed her the fishing pole. He showed her how to take in the fishing line. He took the live fishing bait box, pulled out a worm and handed it to her. Mary screamed so loud Mike's father almost fell off the stool he was sitting on. "What is that?!" she said disgusted by the creature she had just seen. "It's your bait," Mike said. "It's what you use to lure the fish to the hook." "Don't let it get near me!" she said as she couldn't even look at the box with worms. Mike shook his head and laughed at her cowardice. "Come on, okay, I will hook the bait, then I will show you how to throw it out." Mike hooked the bait and handed Mary the fishing pole. She tried not to look at the bait as she with Mike's help tried to throw it into the river. Mike's father gave her the fishing stool and sat down on the grass beside her as they were waiting for her to catch something for the first time. Enjoying the peaceful and serene moment Mary said, "You know what would be perfect right now? A Starbucks Pumpkin Spice Latte." It didn't take long before she was getting bored of just sitting there watching the fishing pole, but she didn't have to be bored for long before the fishing pole and line started moving. "I think you caught something there Mary," Mike's father Joe said as he pointed towards the fishing pole. "Oh! What do I do?" she said. Mike helped her hold the fishing pole as they pulled up a medium sized trout. "I caught a fish!" she said excited as she almost jumped up and down. "That's just beginners luck." Mike teased. "Now you just have to remove the fish from the hook and kill the fish," he said. "What?" Mary said, almost as if she didn't know that's how fishing works. "You really haven't fished before have you?" Mike's father said teasingly. As Mary couldn't do it, Mike did the job of killing the fish by smashing its head to a stone as Mary looked away, feeling sorry for the little fish. "I thought you wanted to fish, but you're letting me do all of the hard work," Mike said as he and his father looked at each other and smiled as they thought it was funny.

Later that evening, Mike's mother made fresh trout for dinner. Mary had learned that day, that cleaning fish wasn't her thing, as Mike's mother had tried to teach her how to do it. After they were done eating dinner, Mary helped Mike's mother Susan with the dishes, as the men went into the living room watching a sports game. When it was time to go to bed, Mike's parents went to their bedroom and Mike and Mary went to Mike's childhood room, which hadn't changed much since he lived there when he was a teenager. Straight across the room, there was a wooden desk with an old computer and a lamp. Above the desk there was a window, which gave them a view to the backyard of the house which was mostly grass and surrounding trees. To the right was a TV table with a big old television and to the left was a king size bed. His bed was covered with a blue and white bed quilt. As they were lying on the bed, getting ready to sleep Mary looked around the room at all the posters of celebrities and sports teams and photos of Mike when he was young. She wondered if they got children, would they look like Mike or her? What would they call their children? Was she ready to be a mother? Mike went through his old cassette tapes and found one he liked and put it into his old cassette player. "You still have cassettes and a cassette player?" Mary mocked him and said. "You know there's another invention called mp3's right?" Mike ignored her mocking and comments and pressed the play button on the cassette player. A Kenny Rogers song called "Lady" started playing. He started singing along quietly. "Lady, I'm your knight in shining armour, and I love you..." Mary interrupted his singing. "Oh, I've heard this song before! It's a reggae song." "A reggae song? This is not reggae, this is Kenny Rogers," Mike said. "I like the reggae version better. This version is boring. My grandfather likes Kenny Rogers; he's 85," Mary said. "Are you mocking my taste in music?" Mike said pretending to be angry. "Well I'm going to get you for that," he said and tickled her until she couldn't take it no more. "Now come here and dance with me," he said dragging her out of the bed and held her hand and slow danced with her. "Well look who's suddenly being romantic," she said. "Look who's finally not nagging me all of the time, so I want to be more romantic," he replied. Mary wanted to say something smart back, but couldn't and just put her head on his shoulder. She looked up at him. "I like this new and improved Mike." "I like this new and improved us," Mike answered.

Andrew's Dinner with Jennifer's Parents

Andrew had proposed to Jennifer that day, the last time they'd met. She hadn't been ready to give him an answer, but she loved the ring so much that she had kept the ring on her finger and Andrew was hopeful. She had wanted them to do one more thing together before she gave him her final answer. She wanted him to come and eat dinner with her family. She was also hoping to get her parents to accept him, as that would be a sign to her that they were meant to be together. She was hoping for some kind of sign that would give her the assurance she needed, to know for sure that this was the man she was meant to marry. They met in the park and gave each other a hug as they greeted each other. "I bought you these flowers and this gift," Andrew said as he handed her a bouquet of pink roses, which was her favourite. "Wow, thank you Andrew. What is in the gift?" she said. "You have to open it to find out," Andrew replied. They sat down on a bench in the park. "You can open the gift now if you want to," Andrew said. Jennifer slowly removed the dark purple ribbon of the square white gift box. She then removed the wrapping paper and found a necklace. She took it out of the box and looked at it closer and saw that there was an inscribed text on the necklace and she read the text out loud. "A-ni-o-hev-o-takh. It means 'I love you' in Hebrew. Oh Andrew... it's beautiful," she said staring at it. Andrew was happy to see her reaction, but he had even more things to share. "So I've studied the conversion process from my religion to yours. I know it's a complicated process, but I'm willing to do it. That's how much you mean to me." Jennifer didn't say anything, she just hugged him. They were hugging as if they were catching up for all of the years they'd lived together without doing so. Suddenly it was as if the sky opened up and it started pouring down with rain. Jennifer suddenly got worried. She had been waiting for a sign; what if this was a bad sign? What if this meant that God didn't want them to marry? "I brought an umbrella," Andrew said and opened it up above them both. "I checked the weather and knew it was going to rain, so I brought one," Andrew said as Jennifer put her head on his shoulder. She didn't say anything, but she didn't have to. He could tell that she felt safe and comfortable with him. Not long after the short pouring of rain, a double rainbow appeared on the sky. Now that was a good sign; that Jennifer was sure of.

Jennifer and Andrew took the subway to the neighbourhood where her parents lived and they were walking hand in hand. "I like this holding hands thing," Andrew said as he was smiling content. "I could get used to this," he said. "Enjoy it while you can, because when we come closer to my parents' house we can't be seen holding hands. If my parents or their friends see us holding hands, you can forget getting their approval," Jennifer said. "They're really that strict?" Andrew said surprised as where he came from, holding hands weren't such a big deal. They were walking past small brick houses with brown fences and well-kept gardens as Jennifer quickly let go of Andrew's hand. "They live over there," Jennifer said as she was pointing towards a house at the end of the street. When they arrived at the house, they knocked on the door and Jennifer's mother Rebekah opened up, she smiled and hugged them both and was clearly happy to see them. They stepped inside the house and after showing Andrew around the house, they all gathered in the kitchen to eat dinner. They were all sitting around the dinner table engaging in casual conversation. Jennifer's mother asked Andrew if he had ever tried Jewish kosher food. She also asked him about his parents and his upbringing. Jennifer's father was mostly silent, making it obvious that he wasn't a big fan of Andrew. Then there was a moment of silence and Andrew saw his moment to show Jennifer's parents that he was the right one for her. He had done some research which he thought might change how they felt about him as a person and as a potential husband to their daughter. He now had the chance to make a better "first impression" on them. This time he was prepared. "Thank you for inviting me Mr. and Mrs. Rosenberg. I really appreciate it; and to show you my appreciation I brought you a few gifts." Andrew took out a wrapped bottle of kosher wine and handed it to Jennifer's father Abraham, then he handed her mother Rebekah a small gift box. "Thank you Andrew, that was very nice of you," Jennifer's mother said as she looked at Jennifer's father as to make him soften up. Her father seemed to take the hint and made an effort to be a bit more welcoming to their guest. Rebekah opened the gift box and smiled with amazement. "This is beautiful Andrew! Where did you get this?" Andrew was content with her reaction. "The decoration is imported from Israel. The Hebrew text is a house blessing, customized especially for your family," Andrew said. "That was really thoughtful of you Andrew," Rebekah said while she looked at Abraham, as if to say "see I told you so, he isn't so bad." Andrew was pleased, but he wasn't the only one who was pleased. Jennifer was also pleased and content, not only with her parents reaction, but also with Andrew's effort, thoughtfulness and consideration. He had really thought this whole thing through and had put a lot of effort into it. She could see that her parents were softening up. She already knew her mother was easy to convince. Her mother had been waiting for grandchildren for so long now, that she would accept Jennifer marrying just about anyone; even a non-Jew. They were enjoying themselves and everything was going well. Andrew still wasn't finished with trying to impress Jennifer's parents; he knew that Jennifer's decision would ultimately be affected by her parents' opinion and acceptance of him. He wanted to be sure that they truly accepted him. He knew that there was only one thing that would make them truly accept him; and that was if he was a Jew. Andrew had done some research on his ancestry and he had discovered something interesting. He took out the documents he had brought with him and held them in his hand. "I have something to share with all of you," he said. Jennifer looked at him with a questioning look as she didn't know what he was about to reveal. "So I did some research on my family and on my bloodline. I took this genealogy DNA test and I got these test results back," Andrew said as he handed the documents over to Jennifer. Her face lit up with joy as she was reading the documents. "Wait, what? You're Jewish?!" Jennifer felt a mix of shock and excitement. "Well at least partially. When I did the research I found out that I have Jewish ancestry from my mother. It might explain why I've felt so at home with the Jewish religion and with your daughter," Andrew said as he now looked directly at Jennifer's parents and as he took Jennifer's hand and held it tightly. "I love your daughter Mr. and Mrs. Rosenberg, I really do, and there's no doubt in my mind that she is the right one for me. There's nothing else I want more than to marry her and make her my wife, but I really respect you and want your blessing. I also know that Jennifer highly regards your opinion and that your approval of us may determine the fate of our future together." Andrew looked at them hoping that they would accept him, accept them together and give them their blessing.

At a Church in the South

Mike didn't really want to leave his parents' house or the South, but they had jobs to go back to, so they had to. The weekend had gone by so fast and it was already Sunday. Mike's parents had finally convinced him and Mary to come to church and join the morning service, before they went home. It wasn't only his parents' eagerness to get him to join that had made him come. He himself wanted to come, as he felt he needed to get right with God about something he had done. Mary wasn't difficult to ask, as she had become increasingly religious and interested in God and religious stuff after the accident. She had been listening to sermons and reading the Bible a lot more lately. When they arrived at church they all sat down in the church pew. When the entire congregation had sat down, the Preacher started to preach. "Then God created the man and the woman. He created the woman out of the man's rib. He called the man Adam and the woman Eve. He gave them a wonderful life together in the Garden of Eden, in Paradise. They were enjoying the beauty of marital bliss, but what happened? Temptation came. A serpent whispering sweet lies; making them think they were missing out on something better. Then Eve ate of the apple and Adam did too, and then what happened next? The shame and blame game. The woman said, 'The serpent made me do it.' The man said, 'That woman you gave me made me do it.' It was always someone else's fault, always pointing fingers at somebody else. We can see the same thing today in marriages and relationships. 'I'm unhappy because he or she doesn't do this or that.' The Bible says to husbands to love their wives as themselves, and to women to submit themselves to their husbands. It's when we go out of the will of God and stop following his advice we start experiencing trouble. Jesus also experienced temptation. The devil told him; 'all of these things I will give to you, if you just compromise and do this one thing God told you not to do.' Now Jesus passed the test, but how many people are there today who are willing to compromise God's will to get what they want? The Bible says that God hates divorce and that adultery is a sin, and this is the subject of today's sermon. I've heard that some of you in our congregation are considering divorce. Now I know marriage can be hard; it takes a lot of hard work to make it work. Love is like a rose, it has beautiful flowers and yet it also has thorns. And as Abraham Lincoln said, 'We can complain because rose bushes have thorns, or rejoice because thorn bushes have roses.' You can focus on what your partner does wrong or what he or she does right. Now, some of you may relate to what Paul said in Romans 7:15. He said, 'I don't really understand myself, for I want to do what is right, but I don't do it. Instead I do what I hate.' It's a constant struggle to choose what's right over wrong. You want to do right, but then you mess up and make mistakes. So what do you do when you mess up, make mistakes and do the wrong thing? You confess and repent. You confess your sins, by coming clean and telling the truth about the sins you've committed and the things you've done wrong. Then you have to be genuinely sorry for the wrong you've done. Now I feel it so clearly, that God is telling me that someone here in this room has done something wrong, and that it's time to tell the truth. It's time to come clean and confess your wrongdoing, so your conscience can be clean." After the words of the Pastor, Mike was convinced that he had to confess and repent, if he wanted forgiveness from Mary and also from God. He knew he had to tell Mary the truth about what had happened.

Mike's Confession

Mike and Mary had come home from visiting his parents and they were sitting on the couch, resting after a long day of driving and unpacking. That's when Mike chose to come clean about what he had done. He confessed to her that he had gone out with Carla again a few weeks ago. He knew that he should have deleted her number a long time ago, but maybe he had become too accustomed to Carla's compliments and admiration of him. She had made him feel important and as if he was good enough, but it still didn't justify what he had done. He had taken her home that day, following her to the door. Carla had kissed him on the cheek and had almost convinced him to join her in, but he had stopped it there. He knew right there and then that it was wrong, that he had to go home to his wife. He could have done more wrong than what he did, but he didn't. He knew that there wasn't an excuse that could justify his behaviour, and he wondered if Mary could ever trust him or forgive him again. Knowing that Mike had done the same thing again, was too much to handle for Mary. Mike had known how much it had hurt her the first time, and then he had done the same thing again? Mary was furious and couldn't even look at Mike; she knew she just needed to get out of there. She needed a break, not only from Mike, but from everything. Without looking at Mike or saying a word to him, she went out of the living room and upstairs to the bedroom. Mike sat in the living room with his face in his hands, knowing that he had really messed up. He didn't know that Mary was upstairs packing her things. Mary had found a few basic items and clothes to bring with her and had packed lightly. She locked the suitcase, went downstairs to the hallway and put on her jacket and shoes. She was just about to walk out the door, when Mike stopped her with his hand. "Where are you going? Are you leaving? Please don't go Mary. I've said I'm sorry; I will do what I can to make you trust me again. I can quit my job and find another place to work, if that's what it takes."

Mary firmly removed Mike's hand from her arm. "Mike, I've already decided that I will go, there's nothing you can say that will change my mind," Mary said in a calm and cold tone. Mike was used to Mary getting all emotional, but this was a new side of Mary he wasn't used to. He almost wanted her to be all emotional like she used to be. At least that way he would know that she still cared. "Bye, Mike." Mary grabbed her suitcase and walked through the entrance door. Mike watched her as she walked to the car, got in and then drove away. Mike wasn't the type of man that showed emotions. However he found it difficult to hold back the tears that were gathering in the corner of his eyes. Knowing how stubborn Mary was, he wasn't sure if she would take him back this time and give him another chance. Mike stood in the entrance door looking for a long time, hoping her car would come back and park in the driveway. He hoped that she would come back and hug him and say that she couldn't do it, that she just couldn't leave; but it didn't happen. He closed the door and went to the living room and looked around. The house felt emptier than ever, without the presence of his wife. She's the one who made the house a home, who filled the house with her laugh and sometimes childlike behaviour. Her perfume was still lingering in the air and he looked at the photos of them that were on the wall over the fireplace and all of the decorations that Mary had placed on it. The radio was on in the background playing a song by Chris Young, with lyrics describing exactly what he was feeling.

"God, I'm down here on my knees, because it's the last place left to fall. Beggin' for another chance, if there's any chance at all. That you might still be listening, loving and forgiving guys like me. I've spent my whole life getting it all wrong, and I sure could use your help cause from now on. I want to be a good man, and do like I should. I wanna be the kind of man the mirror likes to see. I wanna be a strong man and admit that I was wrong.

God I'm asking you to come change me to the man I wanna be. If there's any way for her and me to make another start, could you see what you could do, to put some love back in her heart, cause' it's going to take a miracle, after all I've done to really make her see, that I wanna be a stay man, I wanna be a great man. I wanna be the kind of man that she sees in her dreams...

As Mike was listening to the song he reminisced all their good memories, and at the same time remembering and regretting all of the mistakes he had made. He hadn't prayed in a long time, but this time he humbled himself and said a silent prayer to God and hoped he would bring his wife back.

A Biblical Love Story about Patience

Jennifer and Andrew were sitting in Jennifer's apartment and were reading the Torah together. Jennifer had eventually said yes to Andrew's proposal. That day after they had been at her parents' house, she knew that Andrew was the man she wanted to spend her life with. On their way home they had walked through the same park where they had seen the double rainbow earlier that day and Jennifer had stopped him in the middle of the park. She embraced Andrew for a long time before she looked at him and told him. "My answer is yes. Yes I'm ready to be yours and yes I want to be your wife." As they kissed for the first time, the rain poured down from the skies, but they both ignored it as they knew that it was a moment they would cherish forever. As they were now engaged and about to get married they had to make some preparations. One of those preparations was Andrew's conversion to Judaism. Andrew was in the process of converting to her Jewish religion. She was helping him with studying the Scriptures. She started reading to him from a chapter in Genesis 29.

"Now Laban had two daughters; the older was named Leah, and the younger was named Rachel. Leah had weak eyes, but Rachel was shapely and beautiful. Since Jacob loved Rachel, he answered, "I will serve you seven years for your younger daughter Rachel." Laban replied, "Better that I give her to you than to another. Stay here with me." So Jacob served seven years for Rachel, yet it seemed but a few days because of his love for her. Finally Jacob said to Laban, "Grant me my wife, for my time is complete, and I want to sleep with her." So Laban invited all the men of that place and prepared a feast. But when evening came, Laban took his daughter Leah and gave her to Jacob, and he slept with her. And Laban gave his servant girl Zilpah to his daughter Leah as her maidservant. When morning came, there was Leah! "What have

you done to me?" Jacob said to Laban. "Wasn't it for Rachel that I served you? Why have you deceived me?" Laban replied, "It is not our custom here to give the younger daughter in marriage before the older. Finish this week's celebration, and we will give you the younger one in return for another seven years of work." And Jacob did just that. He finished the week's celebration, and Laban gave him his daughter Rachel as his wife. Laban also gave his servant girl Bilhah to his daughter Rachel as her maidservant. Jacob slept with Rachel as well, and indeed, he loved Rachel more than Leah. So he worked for Laban another seven years."

"So first he waited seven years for Rachel, and then worked seven more to get her?" Andrew shook his head. "That Jacob guy, he sure was a patient guy," he said. "Just like you," Jennifer said looking at him and admired her soon-to-be husband. She looked at Andrew and smiled, but as she was starting to realize the sacrifice he had made for her and the one he was about to make, her smile faded into seriousness. "Are you sure you want to do this Andrew? Jewish religion is complicated; there are so many rules, laws and traditions…." Andrew put his hand on her hand. "I'm sure. There's not a doubt in my mind. This is what I want to do." Jennifer looked at the man she was about to marry, how much he had grown from that awkward little boy, and how he had turned into the man she had always wanted and needed. She touched his face, feeling his masculine facial features. He softly kissed her hand and the engagement ring she was wearing. He looked at her. He tried to focus on the Torah, to try to distract himself from the tension that was growing between them. "This waiting thing is so difficult," she said. "I know," he replied. They looked at each other for a long time, until Andrew took her hand and gestured for her to stand up. There was music playing in the background and he pulled her towards him, and they slow danced on the spot. Jennifer had her head on his shoulder. Andrew awkwardly tried to find the right place to hold his hands. They looked at each other again. As they danced, they listened to the lyrics of a song by Josh Turner. *"I wouldn't be a man, if I didn't feel like this. I wouldn't be a man, if a woman like you was anything I could resist..."* They danced for a while until Andrew knew that it was time to go, before they did something they would both regret. "I should go Jennifer." Andrew stopped dancing and put her hands down. "I don't want us to do anything we regret. I want to make sure our wedding day and wedding night is everything you have planned and want it to be," Andrew said and Jennifer agreed that it was best to stop it right there. She followed him to the door and they hugged for a long time, before he kissed her on the cheek and was about to go. She didn't want to let go of his hand, and he didn't want to let go of hers, but they knew that they had to let go and eventually said goodbye. Then Andrew went out to the street to walk to the subway. He listened to music on his phone with his earphones plugged in. The music in his ears blocked out the noise of the world as he was walking down the street. As Andrew was walking, he was in his own thoughts as he saw couple's embracing, walking together holding hands. Memories about him and Jennifer were circling around his mind. How happy he was now that they were finally engaged and about to get married. Tomorrow was a big day, as it was the day of his conversion and he had to go home and get some rest. He listened to the lyrics of a song which said, *"the longer the waiting, the sweeter the kiss."* He knew that Jennifer was worth the wait.

It was the next morning and the Rabbi looked at Andrew with a serious face. "So are you sure you want to do this Andrew? Are you willing to follow the Torah all of the decrees, laws and take on the yoke of the commandments and to be fully bound by them, for the rest of your life?" "Yes I am." Andrew answered holding his hand on the Torah. There was not a doubt in his mind that this was the right thing to do, that Jennifer was worth it. Whatever he had to sacrifice to be with her, he would do it. Not only that, he had also started to become increasingly interested in Jewish religion and he genuinely wanted to get to know the religion of his ancestors. He wanted a closer relationship with God, just as much as he wanted a relationship and marriage with Jennifer. The Rabbi put the Jewish cap called Kippah on his head. "Congratulations Andrew, you are now fully conversed and accepted into our Jewish community." Andrew had finally finalized his conversion. He had studied the Torah daily, he had learned about the 613 commandments. He had taken a bath in something called a mikvah. He had learned the prayers and the blessings that were to be said for the Sabbath, the wine, the bread, for washing the hands and so many other things. He now understood what Jennifer meant when she said that her religion was complicated with lots of rules, rituals and traditions. He still wouldn't want it any other way; it was a price worth paying to be with her. Not only that, he finally felt like he had found the right path in life and like he was getting closer to the person he was destined to be. He couldn't wait to start a new life with Jennifer as her husband, and eventually build a family with her.

Chapter 6

Saying Goodbye to Mistakes

Mike had messed it up again and he knew it, and he was reminded of his mistakes daily at work, as Carla was in the same building. One day as he was walking past Carla's office, he saw that she was packing her things in boxes. He was trying to stay away from her and made it a point not to talk with her, but she saw him before he managed to walk past her office unnoticed. "Hey Mike. Aren't you going to say goodbye to me, before I leave?" Carla said. "Are you leaving?" Mike said looking confused. "Yes I'm moving out of the city, headed for a better life in California she said. I always wanted to try acting and this office thing isn't really for me. And where do you go if you want to be a star? I'm going to where the opportunities are. I'm getting older. I don't have more time to waste, sitting around and waiting for opportunities to come to me, or waiting for men to make up their minds about who they really want to be with," she said looking directly at him. "So to answer your question Mike, yes I'm leaving. Say hi to your girl and congratulate her from me, because she's the one who got you; she's one lucky girl." Carla took her box, and got out of the office. Mike couldn't find the right words to say, so he was just standing there as he was watching her walk away. Just as he saw the mistake of his life walking away, the opportunity of his life showed up tapping at his shoulder. "Hey Mike. She's nice to look at isn't she?" his boss John said as he had obviously seen Mike staring at Carla as she was walking away. "Too bad she had to leave. She said she was leaving for California, she want to chase her dreams or something. Don't they all?" John said and laughed. "But that's not what I wanted to talk with you about Mike. Do you have time to come into my office?" Mike followed him to the office where the walls were covered with brown wooden panels and a brown leather chair that made the office look like it was from another decade. He sat down in the chair and looked around. On the walls there were pictures of his family. "Beautiful family you have there," Mike said. "Thank you Mike. Do you have any children yourself?" his boss John replied. "No not currently, not yet," Mike replied, feeling uncomfortable, not being sure why he was there. Was he about to get fired? Had Carla said something to get revenge?

Come My Beloved, to Meet the Bride

Andrew was standing in front of the mirror, in the room that was reserved for the groom on his wedding day. Today he was the groom and Jennifer was the bride. The day of their wedding had finally arrived. He was trying to straighten his tie, but he was nervous and his hands were shaking slightly. He was wearing his new Kippah on his head, trying to get used to it as Jennifer's father Abraham straightened it and fixed it in the right place. "That's how you should wear it. Now it's in the right place. So now you're one of us Andrew. You really love my daughter don't you?" Abraham said. "Yes sir, I really do," Andrew said as he took one last look in the mirror. "It's time to go out there now, the ceremony is about to start," Abraham said as he gathered his camera and got ready to go out to where the wedding ceremony would take place. Jennifer had wanted an outdoor wedding, but was worried about the weather and if it would be good enough for the ceremony. She looked out of the window and looked at the skies which weren't looking promising. She really wanted an outdoor wedding, but she didn't want rain on her wedding day. She worried about her make-up and the guests if it were to rain, even though they had put up tents above the chairs where the guest would sit and a chupah, a decorated tent, where they would be exchanging the vows. Not long after she had the thought, the rain started pouring down all over the city. And the ceremony was just about to start. Jennifer sat in front of the mirror and looked at herself and reminded her to take a deep breath. This was her day; this was the moment she had been waiting for, for a long time. She didn't want anything to ruin her mood, not even a little bit of rain. Her mother came into the room and interrupted her thoughts. "Are you ready to go and meet your soon-to-be husband?" she said. "Yes I'm ready mom," Jennifer answered as she straightened up her dress, and made sure that her hair and lipstick was just right for this moment. She hadn't seen Andrew in a week, and knew that she was more than ready to see him. In Jewish religion a bride and groom was likened to a King and Queen, and royalty always had an entourage following them. The entourage following her to her husband was her own two parents and they were walking beside her. She was now ready to walk towards her soon-to-be husband. Jennifer saw the Rabbi through the veil that was covering her face. The Rabbi started speaking. "So Rebekah immediately dismounted from her camel and asked the accompanying servant who he was. When she heard that this was her future husband, she modestly covered herself with a veil. Isaac brought her into the tenth and married her." Jennifer knew that it was her cue to start walking. Luckily the rain stopped right before she was about to go and meet her groom. Then the song they had chosen for the ceremony started playing. It was a Hebrew song which translated into "Come my beloved, to meet the bride." She looked around the crowd, breathing in the fresh air coming from the recent rainfall. Andrew looked at her, and then she looked at him, smiling from ear to ear. She looked around at the happy faces of everyone in the crowd and she started walking step by step towards Andrew. She looked around at the guests who were smiling at her, waving and taking photos. It all happened as if it was in slow motion. She couldn't believe that the moment was finally here, that moment she had been waiting for, for such a long time. She paused for a moment to take it all in, and then continued walking. She could feel happy tears coming down her face, but tried to control herself to not ruin her make-up. She looked at Andrew dressed in a suit, wearing his kippah on his head. He smiled and she could see how happy he was to see her. They looked each other up and down and smiled at each other. She continued walking towards him. She finally arrived to the chupah tent, where he was standing. She smiled at him as she circled slowly around him seven times as was the custom, as to create an invisible wall around them. For a moment it was as if it was only those two alone, as if time was standing still for them to enjoy. When she had circled him seven times, she stopped and stood beside him. The Rabbi was standing in front of them. As the Rabbi was about to speak, a double rainbow appeared in the sky; as if it was sign from above, blessing their union of marriage. The Rabbi started speaking. "May God's blessings be upon this union; may this divine moment be graced with His divine presence. 'Kiddushin' means sanctification, signifying the uniqueness of the Jewish marriage where God himself dwells, in the home, and the relationship is elevated to another level of holiness. We are gathered here today to sanctify the union between Jennifer and Andrew, to make two single souls become as one. In the Torah we read that Adam said, 'This is now bone of my bones and flesh of my flesh; she shall be called woman, for out of man she was taken. For this reason a man will leave his father and his mother and be united to his wife, and they will become one flesh.'" The Rabbi held up a cup of wine, recited a blessing and thanked God for sanctifying the marriage. Jennifer and Andrew both took a sip of the cup. The Rabbi turned towards Andrew, who was new to these Jewish marriage rituals. "Andrew you can now put the ring on your bride." Andrew was smiling as the crowd was cheering him on. Andrew had practiced the line he was told to say, as he was putting the ring on his bride. "With this ring you are consecrated to me, according to the law of Moses and Israel." His hands were shaking from being nervous as he put the ring on Jennifer's finger. This was all so new and different to him and he was hoping he was doing everything right. Jennifer and Andrew read the "Ketubah", which was a Jewish marriage contract and agreement between a husband and a wife. Andrew read his part. "I will work, honour, feed you and support you in the custom of Jewish men, who supports their wives faithfully." The Rabbi once again blessed the wine and they drank of it as the Rabbi spoke. "As you are now drinking of this wine your souls are now being reunited, as you were before you entered this world.

May your souls experience the same delight in each other now, as you did before you entered this world in the pristine primal state, in the Garden of the Eden." The Rabbi then wrapped a cup in a large cloth napkin and placed it under the foot of Andrew. Andrew stomped and shattered the glass and everybody shouted "Mazel Tov." The Rabbi then ended the ceremony with a few final words. "You have now become one flesh as husband and wife. Marriage is about learning to put each other first, to make compromises. Andrew here has made a big compromise, by converting into the Jewish religion. The real test starts now, as marriage is a lifelong commitment to be willing to be accommodating to each other's needs and wants. As you are now starting your lives together, I will end this ceremony with a blessing and a prayer. 'May the Lord bless you, keep you, make His face shine upon you and give you peace.'" Everybody clapped cheerfully for the newlyweds, as Jennifer and Andrew were now husband and wife.

Mike's New Opportunity

Mike looked at his boss John. "The reason I wanted to talk with you Mike, is because I have a job offer for you," John said. "A job offer? Mike said confused. "What kind of job offer?" "Well. My job," John said firm as if it was the most natural thing to say. "Your job?" Mike almost stuttered as he could barely speak. He was shocked and a bit confused, questioning whether he had heard his boss right or not. "Sorry sir, not to be disrespectful, but what makes you think that I would be fit for your job? I don't have the experience, I haven't…." John stopped him in the middle of his sentence. "Mike, you remind me a lot about me when I was younger. One day I got my lucky break, someone saw potential in me, and saw what I could be if I was given the chance. My life would have been very different, hadn't it been for that one person who believed in me. My marriage was almost falling apart back then. Me and my wife were having lots of arguments about money as we were struggling, and were trying to make ends meet with my low paying job. When I got the job offer, my life changed. Not only did my pay check improve, but my marriage was saved also. I could finally be the provider and the man she needed me to be. I could do things for her, which I only could dream of doing before that. My children got better lives because of it and I could also help other people. What I'm trying to say is that I believe you will be fit for this job, not because of your experience, but because of your personality. You're like me Mike, you have a lot of potential. You just haven't gotten a fair chance to use it yet, until today. I'm retiring in a few months, and I need someone I can trust to take over for me. I trust you Mike, I believe you are the right man for the job. If you want it, the job is your Mike; a better office, better pay and a better life. What do you say?"

I Am My Beloved's and My Beloved Is Mine

Jennifer and Andrew were enjoying their wedding day. The wedding reception was indoors in a place Jennifer and her mother had spent days decorating. The white chairs were decorated with gold coloured ribbons. There was music playing in the background, which Jennifer and Andrew had chosen together ahead of the reception. People were dancing, some were drinking and sitting around the tables talking, laughing and enjoying themselves. The children were running around playing and using the place as one big playground. Jennifer couldn't be happier as she was starting her new life with her husband. When it was time for dinner they sat next to each other enjoying a delicious meal, exchanging long looks. After eating dinner they ate the wedding cake, and some of the guests were standing up to make speeches. Andrew was getting a bit tired, it had been a long day. He was tired, but a happy man knowing that he had married the right woman. Andrew and Jennifer were slow dancing as they were looking into each other's eyes. Their song 'I wouldn't be a man' was playing in the background. Andrew touched Jennifer's face. "I can't believe that this moment has finally arrived. I've wished for this for so long. To be married to you, to call you my wife. There were times I started doubting if it would ever happen, but here we are together as husband and wife." Andrew was experiencing a mix of marital bliss and tiredness after the long day. His hands were tired after all of the shaking hands with the gusts, and his facial muscles were tired of all of the smiling. His feet were tired after all of the standing in uncomfortable shoes. His eyes were tired after waking up early and it was now getting close to midnight. He was tired, but at the same time he didn't want this night to end. Not long after midnight one guest after another was heading home, the parents who had been there with small children had already left. Eventually it was only Jennifer and Andrew and Jennifer's parents who were left cleaning up the mess. As they were cleaning,

Abraham went up to Andrew and congratulated him and welcomed him to the family. It meant a lot to Andrew to have Jennifer's father approve of him, as he had worked so hard to show Jennifer's father that he was a good man. Andrew was about to tell Abraham how much it meant to him when Jennifer and her mother came towards them. Jennifer's mother also congratulated Andrew. Andrew took his arm around Jennifer and looked at her and her parents, and felt the joy of finally being married to her and being approved by her family. Jennifer's mother looked at the clock and then looked at them. "Now this is your night, and I won't allow you to stay here and clean any longer. You guys go and enjoy your wedding night and we will clean up here." Andrew looked at Jennifer who didn't seem to mind leaving. They both accepted the offer. They hugged the parents and walked out hand in hand. When Jennifer and Andrew finally arrived at the hotel they would be staying for their wedding night, they both kicked off their shoes as the first thing they did. "Ouch, my feet are aching after all of the standing and dancing," Jennifer said as she went to the gold framed mirror in the hallway and looked at herself. After a long day and night, her wedding make-up and hair wasn't as perfect as it had been earlier and for a moment she felt a bit self-conscious. Andrew walked up behind Jennifer and embraced her. He looked at his wife in the mirror, and almost couldn't believe how lucky he was to have a woman like her in his life. He kissed her on her cheek. "You're the most beautiful thing I've ever seen."

Mike Goes to Get His Girl Back Home

Mike had said yes to the new job offer. Now he could finally be the man his wife wanted and needed him to be. He could now take her on a vacation to France, something which she had wanted to do for a long time. It was something which he had wanted to do for her, but hadn't been able to do. He knew he had to go to his wife and tell her the good news and make her come back home with him. He had found out that she was staying at her mother's cabin, which was at a quiet place in the woods. He knew that it was time to go and get his wife home; if he would be able to convince her stubborn self to do so. Mike was sitting in the car driving towards the cabin where Mary had been staying for weeks. The radio was playing for full on his favourite country channel and he was listening to the lyrics as he was driving. Mike was driving to Mary, to get her back and take her home with him; right where she belongs. He knew where the cabin was, as they had spent some weekends there in the summer the previous year. He drove through the dirt road into the woods. When he arrived at the cabin by the lake, he parked his car and turned off the music. Mary was sitting on the porch of the wooden cabin, wearing a long floral dress and a big hat, drinking her tea and writing on her script. Mike looked at her. She looked so serene, content and happy. Maybe this was just what she had needed? Maybe taking a few weeks apart would do them more good than bad? He hoped she had gotten enough time to miss him, and that it would make her long to go home with him. He got out of the car, took off his sunglasses and walked up to the cabin. He stopped in front of the staircase with three steps that led up to the wooden porch where she was sitting. "Hello Mike," Mary said as she was sipping on her tea and reading through her script. "Can I come up and join you?" Mike said. "Sure," she said calmly with her facial expressions revealing nothing about what she was feeling or thinking. Mike then walked up the three steps and sat down on a wooden chair.

"So how you've been? How is life out in the woods?" Mike said. "It's not so bad," she said thinking about all of her daily trips to Starbucks, the take-away food she had been buying and the trips to the mall, which wasn't too far away. She hadn't been living as primitive out there as it could seem like. She took a sip of her tea and looked at her script which was now finished, ignoring Mike's constant staring and attempts to figure out what she was thinking and feeling. She read through the script quietly in her mind. *"She wanted to run up to him and hug him right there and then, but couldn't let herself. She had to control herself and her feelings. She couldn't let him think that what he had done was okay..."* Mike tried to break the silence. "So... What have you been doing while you've been here?" "Not much, just writing my script," she said continuing to look at the script instead of him. Mike knew he had to say something that would make her put down the walls she had put up between them. "Look Mary, I know I've been foolish, I've been dumb and I made the biggest mistake of my life. I've gotten a lot of time to think the last few weeks, and I'm willing to do anything to get you back home with me. I miss you; the house feels empty without you. The house is a mess, I'm a mess. I need you Mary. You're the one who keeps me sane, you're the one who holds it all together and I know that now. I'm sorry that I didn't appreciate you as much as I should have, but I promise that if you come back home with me now I will appreciate you every day. I will love and honour you and be faithful. I will even let you go through my phone every day, and even give you the passwords to all of my accounts and devices if that's what you need to trust me." She was about to take a sip of her tea and stopped when she heard him say that. "You mean all of your accounts and devices? Even Facebook?" she said suddenly paying more attention to what he was saying. "Yes I'll do whatever is necessary. The only thing that matters to me, is that I have you there next to me, every day." Mary took a moment to pause, pretending to be thinking really hard before she answered. "Well okay then, since you put it that way, maybe I can change my mind about staying out here." She got up from the chair, brought her tea and script with her and went inside the cabin without saying anything. Mike looked around confused, not knowing what to do or say. He didn't get time to stay confused for long as Mary came back with all of her suitcases, then locked the door and looked at him. "Are you ready to go?" Mike wasn't sure if he had understood her correctly and didn't want to assume anything. "Go where?" he said. "Go home," she said and started walking towards the car. Mike started walking after her. He wasn't sure what to make of her behaviour. "So you're coming home with me? You forgive me?" he said trying to make eye contact with her, to see if she really meant what she said. "Well yeah, I was getting tired of staying out here anyway. This cabin life isn't for me. I miss my bed, my bathroom. I miss not being around mosquitoes. I had already decided to go back home anyways," she said as she got into the car and put on her seatbelt. "So you were torturing me this whole time with your silence, just for fun?" Mike said a bit frustrated. He was feeling relieved because she was finally coming home, but was slightly irritated. As he had been begging and pleading, she had already in her mind decided to go home with him. As they were driving on the road towards their home, Mike looked at his wife in the passenger seat. He was so content to see her sitting there again, after weeks of not having her there next to him. Yes his wife was emotional, at times annoying and at times drove him crazy, but there was no one that he loved more than that woman sitting next to him.

Home Sweet Home

Andrew and Jennifer were standing in the hallway of the apartment they had shared for so many years. It had now been five months since their wedding, and since then everything had happened so fast, way faster than what they had planned. They had planned to enjoy married life together for a while before they got children, but their plans had been interrupted by the little thing that was growing inside of Jennifer's stomach. Jennifer was standing in front of the mirror admiring her growing belly. Andrew walked up behind her hugged her and touched her now visibly pregnant stomach. "I can't figure out if I look pregnant or just fat. The people who don't know I'm pregnant may think I've been enjoying marital life a little bit too much; through eating," Jennifer said. "You definitely look pregnant," Andrew answered while he was looking at the growing belly, wondering if the baby would look like him. "Well I would have told everyone, if it wasn't for my overly superstitious family. According to my family's superstition it's not good to have a baby shower or figure out if it's a boy or a girl. I'm so curious about the gender that I don't know if I can wait until *he* comes out," Jennifer said feeling both excited and frustrated. "*He*?" Andrew said wondering if he had heard right. "I'm so sure that it's a *he*," Jennifer said touching her stomach. "A son? A mini me?" Andrew said trying to not look too excited. "So what should we call this 'mini-me', if you're right?" Andrew asked. "Isaac. That was my grandfather's name, and he was the kindest man I've ever known. I want that to be his name. What do you think?" Jennifer said looking at Andrew. "I love our son Isaac's name," Andrew said looking at them in the mirror and once again at Jennifer's growing belly. He almost couldn't wait to start this new chapter in their lives. There was nothing Andrew wanted more than to make Jennifer happy. He wanted to give her the best life possible, that's why he almost couldn't wait to share the good news he had and to show her the thing he had planned to surprise her with. A few weeks ago he had received a million dollar offer for a new app which he had designed and developed. It meant a whole new life and a world of possibilities for him, his wife and their baby. Their old apartment was alright, but Andrew wanted something more for his wife and their child. He had secretly planned to buy a house and surprise Jennifer. He knew it was risky to buy a house without telling Jennifer, so he had "fool-proofed" his plan, through looking at houses online with her and asking her what she thought about the houses they were looking at. She didn't know what he was planning, but Andrew could tell which houses she liked the best by her reaction. He had looked at houses in the same neighbourhood where Jennifer's best friend Sarah was living. It was a suburban neighbourhood where there were lots of colonial houses with white picket fences and backyard pools. Jennifer had seemed especially excited about one of the houses, and that's the one Andrew had secretly bought and was going to show her. He had told her that they were going to Sarah's place, which was partially true. What he didn't tell her was that he had a surprise to show her on the way to Sarah's place. Andrew and Jennifer got into their car and started driving towards the neighbourhood where the house was. Andrew already knew where it was as he had already been there a couple of times without Jennifer, to make sure that the house was good enough for them. When they arrived at the place, Andrew parked the car and was ready to surprise her. The realtor was waiting for them outside of the house. "Andrew what are you doing? Why are we stopping here? Aren't we going to visit Sarah? She lives further down the road," Jennifer said as she was confused. "Yes we're going there soon, but first I want to show you something," Andrew said and got out of the car. He went to Jennifer's side, opened the car door and helped her out. He held her hand and made her follow him to the entrance of the house. The realtor welcomed them and gave Andrew the key to the house. "Here you go Andrew. I will let you two take a look around. Let me know if you have any questions." Jennifer was still confused by what was happening. "Andrew what is this?" she said. Andrew took her hand and led her to the inside of the house. "This is our new home."

Mike and Mary Gives Love another Try

Mary was waking up in the bed she had missed so much. She stretched out her hands in the air and yawned. She wrapped her satin robe around her, put on her soft slippers and stood up to walk to the bathroom. She saw Mike's pile of clothes that was on the floor, started picking it up and dropped it in the laundry basket without saying a word to Mike. She didn't give Mike any angry looks and she didn't slam doors or cabinets to show him that she was mad. She didn't nag or complain. She realized how much she had changed as a person and wife. Mike's mess usually disrupted her need for perfection and order, and it would usually make her nag and argue with him. Instead of nagging Mike she went to him and thanked him, for fixing the door handle that had been broken for a few weeks. He hadn't done it right away when she asked him to, but she made it a point to let him do it in his own timing, without nagging him as if she was his mother. "I really appreciate that you fixed that door handle," Mary said as she stroked his arm gently and lovingly. Mike looked at her with a look of appreciation. "You're welcome. I should have fixed it earlier. I know it's been bothering you for some time. It's been bothering me also, but there's just been so much work to do at the office the last few weeks," Mike said as he started to pick up the remaining clothes he had left on the floor and dropped them directly in the laundry basket. He knew his wife hated clutter and he did his best to try to be a little bit more organized. Sometimes Mary was quicker than him and picked things up before he got the chance, but at least he genuinely tried to make an effort to improve himself and to do things she loved. That's why he had bought her flowers. He held the flowers behind his back and tapped Mary on her shoulder as she was making the bed. "Here, these are for you," Mike said as he showed her the flowers. "Oh Mike, you bought my favourite flowers. They're beautiful," Mary said with a big smile and rewarded him with a kiss. Seeing how much joy the flowers gave her, made him wonder why he hadn't made an effort to do something so simple more often. They were both now genuinely making an effort to be more considerate of each other's needs and things were starting to look brighter for them. Maybe their differences weren't so irreconcilable after all. "Look at us now; not nagging or fighting and dropping laundry in the right place. We've come so far the last few months," Mary said. "I know we've come far, but I want to take our relationship even further," Mike said as he was touching her stomach. "I think maybe it's time for us to build a family. I know it's something you've been wanting for a long time. I haven't really been ready until now, because I really wanted to be a good provider for you and our future children. That's how I was raised, and that's what I saw my father do. He took care of my mother and all of us and was the main provider. Now with my new job, I'm in a position where I will be able to provide for us, the way I've always wanted to. I want to build a family with you Mary and I want us to have a new fresh start, as a husband and wife. That's why I want us to renew our vows and ask you; Mary will you marry me again?"

Oh Baby

Jennifer and Andrew were at home in their new house. Everything had gone so fast, from receiving the keys to their new house to moving in. Jennifer had at first been sceptical of everything, mostly because of the cost of the house. She just couldn't believe that Andrew could afford to buy such an expensive house. She didn't want him to use so much money just to please her. She would have been happy with less, as long as she was with him. She was his wife now, and he didn't have to go overboard to impress her or her family. She just hoped that he understood that; but she did love their new home. Andrew was in the room they had chosen to be the nursery for baby Isaac. He was struggling with the flat pack furniture that was supposed to become a chest of drawers for Isaac. He read the assembly instructions and looked at the screws and still weren't able to make the drawers fit right. Jennifer came into the room and looked at all of the screws that were lying around on the floor together with the materials made of dark cherry wood. She looked at Andrew and saw his look of frustration. "You're really screwing this up aren't you?" Jennifer said and laughed as she thought it was a funny joke. "Are you sure you don't want me to call my dad? He's great with these things. He can fix it for us," Jennifer said without realizing that she had just triggered Andrew's fears of being inadequate as a father. Jennifer's comment, Andrew's insecurities and his tiredness from getting the house and everything ready for their baby, weren't the best combination. Andrew snapped back at Jennifer. "You want me to call your father? So he can see how useless and unfit I am for this role I'm about to take as a father. How can I be a good father, when I can't even build this furniture for our son?" Jennifer was taken by surprise by Andrew's angered response. She didn't know that Andrew was feeling insecure about becoming a father. She couldn't understand why, as she knew without a doubt that he would be a great father. "Relax Andrew, I was just joking. I saw you with the screws and just made a bad joke. I wasn't insinuating that you're screwing things up, or that you're less of a man in anyway. I don't know why you're so insecure about this. I know you will be a great father to our son; and you're more than man enough for me, just look at these muscles," Jennifer said as she squeezed Andrew's biceps and smiled at him, trying to make him lighten up. Jennifer put her hands on his shoulders and looked him in the eyes. "Andrew, you're a great husband and you're going to be a great father. Let's build this thing together. I will read the instructions and you can do the building. Alright?" Jennifer's assuring words helped him to calm down a bit. He realized that he may have overreacted a bit. Now he felt bad for letting his frustrations out on her. He embraced her. "I'm sorry Jennifer; it's just been a bit too much lately. This new business deal has required so much of me. That in addition to moving into a new house, trying to fix things up and get things ready before the baby arrives." He sighed as if talking about it helped him release some of the frustrations he'd been carrying on the inside. He looked at Jennifer and the calmness and confidence she seemed to exude. "Why are you so calm about this whole thing? A baby is a huge responsibility." She looked at him and stroked his cheek softly. "Because getting babies and becoming parents has been done since the creation of the world. There's nothing more natural than that." When they worked together as a team, it didn't take long before they were able to finish the chest of drawers made of dark cherry wood. With some good old fashioned teamwork, Andrew and Jennifer had gotten the whole nursery close to being ready for the baby. There was just one last piece of decoration that would make the room complete. Jennifer had ordered a custom made name sign made of wood. The name sign said "Isaac" as they both had agreed on that name. "My father is going to be so happy, when he finds out that we're going to name the baby after his own father." Jennifer looked around the nursery satisfied with how it looked. She had gone with a neutral style with mostly white and cherry wood details. She had bought the softest white blanket, which she had hung over the wooden rocking chair that was in the corner. The baby crib made of cherry wood had a white duvet which was covered with silver stars. On the wall above the bed was the Aaronic blessing in a wooden frame. She looked around the room and then at Andrew. She embraced him and knew that their future together would be bright.

Chapter 7

Vacation in France

Mary was so excited as she and Mike were about to board the plane that would take them to their vacation destination; France. First they would spend a couple of days in Paris, then go to the Southern part of France and enjoy the French Riviera. Vacation to France had always been Mary's dream as she loved everything French; especially French fashion. She couldn't wait to shop and renew her wardrobe with the latest fashion from Paris. Mike wasn't all that enthusiastic about France, he just wanted to make Mary happy; and taking her out on a vacation was a long overdue promise. They landed in Paris and then took a cab to the hotel they would be staying. Mike was carrying all the bags while Mary was carrying her coffee in one hand and shopping bags in the other. When they entered the hotel room, Mary dropped the shopping bags on the floor, went to the bed and dropped down on it. She stretched out her hands and then put her hands behind her head. She looked up to the ceiling and with a childlike enthusiasm and excitement she said, "J'aime Paris!" She sat back up on the bed and looked at Mike. "Don't you just love this place Mike, isn't it amazing?" Mike didn't look as if he was as enthusiastic about France as she was. "It's alright," he answered. Mary was almost offended with Mike's lack of enthusiasm. "Alright? France is more than just alright," Mary said as Mike put away the luggage he had been carrying. He sat down on the bed and turned on the television. Everything was in French. "Maybe I would like it better if I could understand what people here were saying. Doesn't anyone here speak English?" Mary's mood was dampened by Mike's complaining. She stood up from the bed and looked at Mike. "Are you going to complain and be negative the entire time we're here? If so you can just leave, because I'm here to enjoy myself," Mary said with her hand on her hip. Mike rolled his eyes. "You know we're here to renew our vows right? I kind of have to be here, unless you're planning to renew your vows with someone else." Mary wanted to say something rude back to him, but she held her tongue and decided to do what she did best; shopping. "You know what Mike, you can stay here with your negativity and I will leave. I hope your mood is better when I come back from shopping." Mary took her purse put on her high heel shoes and was about to walk out the door when Mike took her hand and pulled her back. "I'm sorry okay? I didn't mean to dampen your mood with my complaining. I was just tired from all of the travelling, carrying all of the bags and I didn't get much sleep last night either. Can you forgive me?" Mike looked at her and stroked her cheek. Mary really wanted this vacation to be a good one, and Mike did seem as if he was sincere with his apology. "Okay Mike, I forgive you."

Baby Bliss

Jennifer had just come home from the grocery store when the contractions had started. She was in the hallway, taking off her jacket and shoes and the water had just splashed onto the dark wooden floors. Andrew was carrying groceries from the car and came in through the door. When he saw the water on the floor and the look on Jennifer's face he quickly understood what had happened. He had hurried upstairs to gather the bag they had pre-prepared for the hospital stay. They both then hurried into the car and Andrew drove to the hospital. Andrew had been nervous on the way to the hospital as Jennifer had been screaming because of the labour pain. He was scared that she would give birth in the car as he had seen in some video clips on the internet. When they had arrived at the hospital, the birth had gone quickly and it wasn't long before they'd held their new baby son Isaac in their arms. Jennifer's parents had arrived shortly after that. Abraham was happy and proud when he found out that his new grandson would carry the name of his own father. After they had been a few days in the hospital they could finally take their new family member home, and show him the room they had worked so hard to prepare for him. Andrew put baby Isaac in the new car seat and fastened the seatbelt. He looked at his son and was sure he had the most beautiful baby in the world. On the way home Andrew looked in the car mirror a hundreds of times to check on Isaac in the back, he almost couldn't believe that he and Jennifer finally had become parents. Jennifer sat in the seat next to him, clearly tired from giving birth, nursing their baby and taking in all of the impressions and experiences of being a new mother. They were both in their own thoughts as they had just experienced the most amazing moment of their lives. Together they had created this little beautiful human being; it was a miracle from above. When they finally arrived home, Andrew parked the car, got out and went to the other side to help his wife out of the car. He then went to the back to take out baby Isaac. Jennifer unlocked the door and they got into the house. This was a whole new beginning for them, and they both were excited about starting a whole new chapter in their lives as a family of three.

Renewal of Vows

Mike and Mary had spent a couple of days in Paris, and after that they had boarded the plane to go to Southern France. When they arrived at the French Riviera they left the bags in the hotel room, changed to beach clothes and went straight to the beach. Mary was wearing a large hat and sunglasses, and a white maxi dress with flowers. "What do you need that large hat for? I can't even see your small head under there," Mike said and laughed. Mary was a bit offended as she thought she looked pretty good. "We'll see if my Instagram followers agree with that. I bet they will love this outfit," Mary said and handed Mike her phone and forced him to take what seemed like hundreds of photos of her. She made him take photos of her in front of the hotel, then in front of the beach and on the sunbed while she was drinking an exotic drink she had ordered. "I thought we were done with photoshoots after you forced me to take hundreds of photos of you in front of the Eiffel Tower. Nobody told me that being a husband meant being someone's personal photographer." Mary took a sip of her exotic drink and then she stretched out on the sunbed. "What? Nobody told you that? Everybody knows that," Mary said. She couldn't remember the last time she had been so happy and relaxed. Mike had also lightened up his mood a bit and had really made an effort to make this vacation a good one for them both.

The next day, Mike had made arrangements for them to have their vows renewed at the beach. Since it was only going to be the two of them, he had hired a guy that would film the whole ceremony. That way they could show it to their friends later. Mike told Mary to close her eyes and guided her towards the beach where he had gotten help with organizing a white tent decorated with purple flowers. There were candle lights and rose petals all around the tent. Music started playing in the background. The priest was waiting on them. Mike guided Mary towards the tent and told her to open her eyes. Mary was both shocked and amazed at the same time as she looked around. It was the perfect romantic setting. The sunset in the background made it even more beautiful. "Mike... It's so beautiful. Have you done all of this?" Mike could see how happy she was. "Well yes; with a little bit of help. I got a bit of help from the hotel staff to set up the tent, and I got a few tips from your friends when it came to the decorations," Mike answered. "Oh Mike, it's wonderful," Mary said still looking around and she almost couldn't believe that Mike had done something so romantic. Mike took her hand and guided her to the priest. After the priest had said his part, Mike put the ring on Mary's finger and kissed her. "I now declare you as my wife, again."

Dinner at Trina's Restaurant
The girls were gathered to eat dinner at Trina's restaurant. Trina was living her best life, with a newly opened restaurant that was all hers, which she had decorated and perfected to the tiniest little detail. She came over to the table where the girls were sitting and sat down with them dangling her hands in front of everyone, to try to get their attention with the big ring that was on her finger. "Trevor and I are getting married next year!" she said excited. The girls were so happy for her. All of the girls had big things to share and talk about. Jennifer had gotten married, moved into a new house and given birth to her son Isaac. Sarah had given birth to her daughter Jasmine. Trina had opened her own restaurant and had finally found the love of her life. Mike and Mary had renewed their vows on their private vacation in France. All of them seemed to be in a good place in their lives. Mary showed the girls photos and video clips from her and Mike's vacation in France. Then Jennifer and Sarah were showing photos of their babies, with all of the girls saying "aww" with every photo. Sarah looked at Mary. "So when are you and Mike getting a baby?" Sarah asked. Mary looked at the baby photos the girls were sharing, and for a moment she felt the pain of not having her own children. "Well, I don't know. We've been trying for a while, and I'm starting to wonder if maybe it just isn't meant to happen for us. Maybe the accident did something to damage my ability to conceive. Either way, we've already decided that we're going to accept what God chooses for us. If we're meant to have a baby, then it will happen." Laura interrupted the conversation to change the topic to something more pleasant. "Girls, I have something to share with you. As you know, me and James we've decided to stick together and try to make things work. Well a part of that decision was James agreeing on my wish to move back to the South, to be close to my family and the place I grew up. I really miss that place and this city life, I just don't think it's for me anymore. So we're

moving, next week." All of the girls were shocked, but especially Mary. "You're moving? Why didn't you tell me sooner?" Mary said as it made her sad to know that her best friend for so many years was going to move so far away. She had become so used to always having Laura close when she needed her there. Mary wasn't ready for a change like this in her life, she liked things just the way they were. Laura saw the sad look on Mary's face. "Why don't you and Mike take a break from the big city life and come and join us? I know Mike loves being in the South, and he grew up not so far away from my childhood home," Laura said to Mary, imagining the two of them sitting on a porch in the South, drinking sweet tea and enjoying the country side. "What me? The big city girl, live in the middle of the woods in the South? Without Starbucks on every corner, take away and shopping malls?" Mary said, hiding the fact that she actually didn't dislike the country side as much as she had in the past. She had actually been fantasizing a lot lately, about her and Mike living a quiet life in the country side, being close to nature and having children of their own who had a large outdoor space where they could play. She had even imagined herself gardening, growing vegetables and having chickens who laid fresh eggs every morning. She didn't know where all of these thoughts were coming from, but she knew that it was a desire that was growing stronger.

Dreams Come True

Mary was on the bed sleeping and she was dreaming again. In the dream she was watching a movie on a cinema screen. On the movie screen she could see her and Mike's house as the screen zoomed out further and further away from it. It zoomed out even further and away from all of the other homes around them, where there were different women who were cooking and cleaning and men who were putting empty milk boxes in the fridge and making messes. Some couples were arguing, while others were cuddling and getting along. The cinema screen eventually faded and then the closing credits showed Mary's name as a screenwriter and producer. Suddenly Mary woke up from the dream, as her cell phone was ringing. She cleared her throat and answered the phone. "Hello?" she said, hoping her voice didn't sound too hoarse after sleeping. "Hello Mary. This is Steve. I'm calling you to let you know that we've gone through your script and we've discussed its potential to become a feature film. The truth is that we love it. The script is great; it has great potential to become a million dollar success. You really did a great job with it. Even though it's a romantic comedy, which is usually mostly appealing to women, you've managed to write this script in such a way that we believe it may be appealing to men as well. We've envisioned it being a great movie to release just before Valentine's day, for couples to watch together. We really believe it can be a great success." Mary was speechless, which was unusual for her extroverted self. After she had ended the conversation with Steve, she sat down on the bed thinking about how great everything had turned out to be. Everything had seemed so dark and impossible at one point, but now things were looking bright. Here she was still married, and not only married but actually happily married. And with her script finally accepted and approved, things were as bright as they could be.

Three Isn't Always a Crowd
Jennifer was cooking in the kitchen as Andrew was playing with their now five months old son. Andrew looked at Jennifer, thinking how beautiful she was and how content he was with his life. He had everything he could wish for and more. He had the woman he had always wanted, a beautiful son, a beautiful house and a successful business. Now they were a family, the three of them. He couldn't imagine things being any better than what it was, until Jennifer interrupted his thoughts. "Andrew, I'm not feeling too well. I've been nauseous all morning and I'm so hungry all of the time and I'm craving all of these weird things, just like when I was…" Jennifer stopped talking for a moment, as if she got an epiphany. "But no, it can't be. I've just…" Jennifer was speechless and didn't know what to say. Andrew looked at her and felt a mix of excitement and dread. Was she pregnant again? Already? A baby was a blessing, but they had just been through a pregnancy and a birth. They had barely gotten any sleep or time to themselves the last few months. They both already felt stretched out enough as it was. Jennifer who was already sleep deprived and tired started to cry. She felt bad about crying, because she knew that a baby was a miracle, something to be happy and grateful for. Regardless, she couldn't control the tears that were coming down her cheeks. Andrew gave baby Isaac a toy he could be occupied with and went up to his wife and embraced her. He had the same worries and fears as her, but knew he had to be strong for his wife who had been a bit more emotional than usual the last few weeks. "Jennifer; everything will be okay. You are a great wife and a great mom. I know you're going to do a great job, if it turns out that you're pregnant and we're having another baby. Besides, wouldn't it be great to give baby Isaac a sibling? Someone to play with? Maybe a 'mini-you'?" Jennifer wiped away the tears and started thinking about having her own 'mini-me'. If they got a girl, she could dress her up in beautiful dresses. She could comb her hair,

just like her own mother did when she was a little girl and go shopping together when she got older. As Jennifer started day-dreaming, the thought of having another baby didn't seem as scary. Maybe it would make their small family even more complete?

A Bun in the Oven

Mary was standing in front of the oven as she was waiting for her apple pie to be ready. She had her hair up in a bun and an apron around her waist. The oven made a sound, to let her know that the pie was ready. Mary opened the oven, took out the pie, put it on the kitchen counter and inhaled the delicious smell. Then Mike came into the kitchen. He had been fishing by the lake that was close to their new house in the country. "Ah, what a heavenly smell," he said as he was bowing down towards Mary's stomach, which was now visibly big. "Don't you agree little man?" he said to the stomach as he was smiling. Mike gave Mary a kiss on the cheek and embraced her. Both of them were as happy as they could be. Mike was finally living in the country side, something he had wanted to do for a long time. Mary had adapted to the peaceful life as well. Maybe that's what she had needed to get pregnant; to slow down and live close to nature in a stress free environment. They had barely lived there for a month, and then she had become pregnant. Mary took two pieces of pie and put them on two plates. She opened the refrigerator and brought out the sweet tea she had made earlier, after the recipe Mike's mother had given her. Mary and Mike brought the plates and the sweet tea outside to their large garden and sat down on a blanket they had prepared there. They enjoyed the pie and the sweet tea while listening to the radio which was playing in the background. When they were done eating, they both laid down on the blanket looking up at the clear blue sky, enjoying the serenity of the moment. Mike listened to the lyrics on the radio. *"Cause who I am with you is who I want to be. You're so good for me. And when I'm holding you, it feels like I got the world in my hand. Yeah a better man is who I am with you."* They both looked at each other and were so glad that they had worked things out. As it turned out, their differences weren't so irreconcilable after all. Through learning to communicate better, compromise and be more adaptable towards each other's needs, their marriage had now been saved. It had been a lot of work, but their marriage was a marriage worth fighting for.

Printed in Great Britain
by Amazon